Mistletoe at the Lakeside Resort

The Lakeside Resort Series (Book 3)

SUSAN SCHILD

Mistletoe at the Lakeside Resort
The Lakeside Resort Series (Book 3)

Editing by The Pro Book Editor
Interior Design by IAPS.rocks
Cover Design by Cover Affairs

ISBN: 978-1-7328249-5-9

Main category—Fiction>General
Other category—Fiction>Women's

First Edition

OTHER BOOKS BY SUSAN SCHILD

Christmas at the Lakeside Resort
(The Lakeside Resort Series Book 1)

Summer at the Lakeside Resort
(The Lakeside Resort Series Book 2)

Linny's Sweet Dream List
(A Willow Hill Novel Book 1)

Sweet Carolina Morning
(A Willow Hill Novel Book 2)

Sweet Southern Hearts
(A Willow Hill Novel Book 3)

For my mother, Kay, the original
adventurous woman and a sweetheart.

CHAPTER 1

JENNY BECKETT WOKE UP IN her little log cabin to the sounds of waves lapping on the shore of Heron Lake and a cool fall breeze wafting in. Was there anything more delightful than sleeping with an open window on a cool night? Smiling, she yawned, pushed her two eighty-pound dogs off her bed where, officially, they weren't allowed to sleep, and slipped on a flannel robe. The temperature was finally dropping, heaven after the steam bath of a summer they'd had. Buddy and Bear pranced, capered, and reared up on their hind legs, play fighting. The drop in temperature always made the dogs friskier. As she scooped chow into bowls, Jenny glanced at the Just a Buck store calendar she kept on her fridge. It was October 15th. Hard to believe how much her life had changed in just one year.

Pouring steaming coffee in an insulated mug, Jenny sighed with pleasure as she took that first sip and reminisced. One year ago today, Jenny had walked into Frank's Friendly Hardware Store and met Luke, the man to whom she was now engaged. At the time, Jenny had been in her early forties with a chip on her shoulder about men and a fierce determination to stay a single gal for the foreseeable future. But then she'd met Luke, an open-faced, good-looking, genuinely kind guy with mesmerizing blue eyes. He'd been Jenny's general contractor and helped her renovate her eight guest cabins. The rest was history.

Jenny held out her left hand, admiring the engagement ring Luke had brought back with him from his trip to Australia. From a mine in Queensland, the dark blue square-cut sapphire was flanked by small diamonds. She adored the ring. When she was outside and no one was looking, Jenny sometimes turned her hand back and forth to watch the sun sparkling off the stones. She still couldn't quite believe she was engaged.

Slipping on a fleece and sweatpants, Jenny grabbed her coffee, let the dogs out for a run, and walked with Levi down to the new pole barn she and Luke had just built for the miniature horse. Jenny scratched the wiry hair on his back with her fingernails while he ate the fine, soft, leafy alfalfa grass mixed hay that he loved. Afterward, the two ambled back home, Jenny still thinking about what a game changer of a year it had been.

Last fall, she'd left her familiar life in the town of Shady Grove and taken a huge and risky leap of faith.

Leaving town with just her dogs, her miniature horse, and a beat-up Airstream trailer, she'd moved here to the Lakeside Resort to make a go of her inheritance, the tiny but tidy log homes that sat in a semicircle facing the blue water of Heron Lake. As she did every morning, Jenny sent up a prayer to her late father Jax for gifting her the Lakeside Resort.

Morning, Daddy. Look at what a quiet, pretty morning it is here on the lake. The water looks navy blue in this light. What do you think of the pole barn? Levi seems to like it, though he'd rather hang with the dogs in my living room. I'll bet you've found new poker buddies up there. I know you're beside me during the day and hope you're still enjoying this property that you loved so. Hope you're happy. Miss you and I'm grateful to you every day for this new life.

Heading back to her cabin, the Dogwood, Jenny saw no lights on in the other seven guest cabins. Good. On Sunday evening, the fit-looking couple who'd reserved the Mimosa had kept their eyes glued to their phones during check-in. Yesterday at 6:00 AM, they'd tooled off in their Toyota RAV4 with their bikes on the back and cycled all day on the trails at nearby Heron Heights Park. Jenny hoped they'd let themselves relax a little more today.

In the past year, Jenny'd had to learn everything about innkeeping in order to keep her business afloat. The first day of vacation, a lot of guests had trouble letting go of their devices, even though the reception at the lake was spotty at best. They overplanned their visit, and a few stayed on the go, but by day two, most seemed to get into the flow of lake life. Guests began to spend more time admiring the lake, breathing in the clean, fresh air, and noticing nature. Yesterday, the older couple in the Hydrangea had sat in chairs reading lakeside, pausing periodically to look at a cardinal at the birdfeeder, watch a fast boat cruising, or track an osprey winging by. They'd brought sandwiches outside and enjoyed their picnic lunch. A getaway at the Lakeside Resort was for taking a break from the busyness and hustle of their real life, and reminding themselves of what was most important, their loved ones, quiet, and the beauty of nature.

Not wanting to wake her guests, Jenny softly called to the dogs but, invigorated by the cool air, they ignored her. Buddy was down by the lake bank on the other side of the property, his nose pressed to the ground. "Buddy, come," she called, quietly but firmly, and waved him in. Pausing a split second to size up how serious she sounded, he loped toward her. Bear emerged from under a shrub, gave himself a vigorous shake, and trotted after him. As Jenny approached her front door, she noticed two new things.

One, there was a goose standing outside of the door of her cabin. Canada geese were as common as waves up here at Heron Lake, but this one was made of concrete, wore a small but jaunty red beret, and had an amiable smile on his face. The cement bird hadn't been there last night before she turned in. Jenny grinned. The Frenchman had to be a special delivery from her best friend, Charlotte.

Poking her head around the corner of her cabin, Jenny smiled. Charlotte's green four-door sedan with the basketball-sized dent in the side was parked at a rakish angle beside the Silver Bullet, Jenny's recently renovated old Airstream. Charlotte's dropping in unexpectedly to spend a night or two or three in the Silver Bullet was not uncommon. Though her friend lived in an apartment over the garage of her parent's grand house in the nearby town of Shady Grove, Charlotte was engaged to the mayor of Celeste, Virginia, and Heron Lake was a good spot in between the two towns. Jenny loved the slumber-party feel of having her friend drop by from time to time for a gabfest and a glass or two of vino.

The second new thing Jenny spotted was the note taped to her door. She'd missed it on the way out. Smiling, she read Charlotte's loopy scrawl.

Good morning, girly girl!!! Ashe and a bunch of other mayors are at a leadership conference in Greensboro all week. I missed you all so I'm popping in. May see you later today after my beauty sleep, but I'll be in and out. Busy as a bee for next few days with new client here at lake. Helping a woman decorate the house that she and her husband just bought. You and your mama ready for our big rummage sale adventure Saturday? Meet y'all at 8:30 AM sharp in the parking lot. Wear comfy shoes. I'll bring energy drinks and power bars to keep us going. XO

PS - Found the precious goose at Habitat. Looked like he belonged here. I'm too good to you, aren't I?

PPS - The little guy was wearing the beret when I found him, but he doesn't seem French to me.

Jenny studied the goose again. The look on his face said he was eager for the day and, though she was no expert, he looked like he was smiling. She decided she liked the goose. Who didn't need another optimistic, plucky friend?

Resting her eyes on the mist rising from Heron Lake, Jenny breathed in the heavenly scent, a mix of water, fresh earth, and wood smoke. She watched the heron who stood peacefully on her dock unfurl its wings and glide gracefully off across the water. Jenny still had to pinch herself to believe she lived in such a serene spot. Last year at about this time, she'd just been dumped by her fiancé and evicted from her chicken coop cottage on the outskirts of Shady Grove. She raised her coffee cup up in the air in a toast. "Thank, you, Daddy,' she said softly. Jax had been a charming scoundrel and a no-show of a father, but he'd sure atoned for being MIA for much of her childhood when he'd willed her these eight rustic guest cottages on Heron Lake.

Jenny gave the lightening skies an appraising look. If the meteorologist at WCNC was right about the ten-day forecast, the week and weekend would be sunny, clear, stunning October days, just the thing for the fall maintenance chores she had to get done over the next few days.

The outing Charlotte had planned for them on Saturday, treasure hunting at the annual Heron Lake Fire Department rummage sale, would be even more fun if the weather was pretty. A thrifty yard sale and secondhand store expert, Charlotte had invited Jenny and her mama to tag along with her while she looked for new finds to incorporate into her interior design and staging business. Jenny glanced at the time. She'd better get a move on. At 7:30, Luke was swinging by on his way to work to drop off the supplies her stepfather, Landis, had suggested she buy. Luke had taken over the day-to-day operations of his family's hardware store after his daddy had had a stroke. Frank had had another mild stroke in September that had affected his speech, but he was well on the road to recovery. The big bag of fescue Luke was delivering would work for fall overseeding, and she really needed the organic milky spore remedy she'd ordered to get rid of the pesky white grubs. The fifteen bags of fresh black mulch would dress up the entrance to her cabin, which served as the check-in area for arriving guests.

When Luke got busy, he forgot to eat. Jenny decided to have breakfast ready for him when he dropped off supplies. He could either have a bite and a quick visit with her or, if he was short on time, eat his breakfast in the truck on the way back to the store.

Humming along to the radio, Jenny put bacon slices on to fry and slipped a pan of biscuits into the oven. Since Luke's daddy's strokes, she was cooking healthier. This morning's bacon was made of turkey instead of pork, and the fat-free buttermilk she'd used for the biscuits browning in the oven made them moist and flaky. She didn't mess with the cheese. No Southern cook worth her salt would use low-fat cheese in a bacon, egg, and cheese biscuit.

Jenny paused to sniff the mouthwatering aromas that filled the air. The kitchen smelled like home. Loosely wrapping the finished biscuits in aluminum foil, Jenny popped them in the still-warm oven. After a quick shower, she slipped on jeans, a lightweight cotton sweater, and lace-up boots. When she heard Luke's truck crunching on the gravel driveway, Jenny felt a happy buoyancy in her chest. Her step light, she walked outside to meet him. In his jeans, work boots, and blue tattersall check shirt, he looked as delicious as the kitchen smelled.

"Mornin', darling,'" Luke said in his gravelly early morning voice and blasted her with those eyes of his that seemed to change color. This morning, they were cornflower blue.

Jenny stepped into his arms and lifted her face for a scorching kiss. Leaning her head against his chest, she gave a happy sigh. Oh, how she loved this man. "I missed you."

"Missed you, too." Luke pulled her closer for one more kiss and let her go. He sniffed the air like Bear did in the morning when he caught the scent of a deer or a fox. "Something smells good."

"I made biscuits for you. Do you have time to eat?"

"I do. Let me unload this truck first. Where do you and Landis want everything?"

"Just leave it right there." Jenny pointed to the gravel area right beside Luke's truck. At Landis's suggestion, she had spent the money on a fancy new ergonomic wheelbarrow slash dolly slash yard cart with a design that was supposed to make hauling 200 pounds as easy as hauling feathers. It made yard work so much easier for Jenny, especially with her tricky back.

Jenny arranged Luke's breakfast on a plate while he made quick work of unloading the truck bed. When he stepped into the kitchen, Bear and Buddy careened in behind him, pushing past him like commuters in a New York subway trying to squeeze into the last car. The dogs caught the back of Luke's knees, and he fell toward Jenny, catching himself before he bowled her over. "Whoa," Luke said ruefully as he took a seat at the kitchen table. "The guys are full of beans this morning."

"Sorry about that. They're all revved up because of the cool snap." Jenny put a plate in front of him and handed him a mug of coffee. Luke took a large bite of biscuit, groaned in pleasure, and gave her his usual compliment. "Jenny girl, you can sure rattle some pans."

"Why, thank you." Jenny flashed a smile at him and slid into the chair across from him. The three animals crowded around them, and when Levi tried to follow the boys underneath Jenny's and Luke's legs, the table shifted precariously.

Luke grabbed her mug of coffee just before it tipped.

"All right, fellas. Out of there," Jenny called in an *I mean business* tone. The three of them came out from under the table and skulked away.

After Luke swallowed another bite, he looked at her thoughtfully. "When we get hitched, we'll need a bigger cabin."

Wilting a little, Jenny felt a stab of sadness. "I hate thinking about leaving this place. The Dogwood has been my little jewel box of a home. After all that mess back in town, I landed on my feet here." Leaning back in her chair, she crossed her arms.

Luke's look conveyed his understanding. "This cabin is just the thing for one person or for folks to have a weekend getaway, but what about full-time life here? Don't know about the practicalities of the five of us living in a 300-square-foot cabin." He sipped his coffee.

Looking around, Jenny tried to see the possibilities in the space but came up empty. The small kitchen, living room, and bath made up the downstairs of the cabin, and she had a small loft bedroom upstairs. That was it.

"Maybe we could move furniture around or..." Jenny trailed off, knowing Luke was right. "I don't think this space would work either," she admitted glumly.

Luke popped a bite of biscuit in his mouth. "On the far side of the property, we could build a good-looking but bigger cabin. We'd have more privacy and more legroom." He gave her a wry smile. "As much as you love me, are you ready to overhear NASCAR or golf on television? How about if you're trying to read and I'm doing woodwork right outside the cabin with power saws and sanders?"

Jenny nodded reluctantly. "Will you draw it up or show me what you're thinking of? Promise me it will be pretty?"

"I will, and I promise," he said and was quiet for a moment. "How's business?"

Jenny topped off his coffee and slipped back into her chair. "I've getting reservations for Thanksgiving, but I have wide open spaces between then and New Year's. I've got a few reservations from folks who stayed with us last year, but too many open cabins. I need to get a newsletter out." Her stomach clutched a little as she thought of the vacancies.

"You'll get more bookings," Luke said encouragingly.

He knew how she'd struggled with getting cabins booked over the last year, her first year operating the Lakeside Resort. "I've been worrying about it, so in the September newsletter and on social media, I kind of alluded to a few big Christmas surprises we were planning but I'm not exactly sure what those surprises are," Jenny said sheepishly. Reaching for the small yellow notepad she kept tucked between the salt and pepper shakers, she showed it to him. It was titled **Ideas and To-Do List for Christmas.** It had nothing written underneath the title.

Luke chuckled. "So you need festive Christmas ideas. I'll give it some thought."

"Please," Jenny said plaintively. "I'm going to ask Mama and Charlotte to put on their thinking caps, too." Her friend's creative approach to problem-solving could border on kooky, but she was often the one that came up with the best ideas.

As Luke finished his second biscuit, Jenny rested her chin in her hand and studied him.

Though as square-jawed and good-looking as ever, Luke had dark circles under his eyes. He looked worn down. Stepping in to manage the family's hardware store, looking after his parents, and being called away for an unexpected work assignment in Australia had all taken their toll. Last month, after Luke had spent months training the manager he and his dad had hired at the store, the fellow had abruptly resigned to marry a woman from Texas he'd met through an online dating site. Now, Luke was training the newly hired manager. "How's the store?" Jenny asked.

Luke patted his mouth with a napkin and pushed his chair back from the table. "The new manager, Tom, is going to work out fine. He's a solid guy with a business background. The customers and employees like him, but he needs more experience in bookkeeping." Reaching out, Luke took her hand and gazed at her. "We've also got a wedding to plan for this spring or summer. Add that to the To-Do List." He tapped the yellow notepad with his forefinger.

"I know. Spring will be here before we know it," Jenny murmured, while trying to decide if the flutter in her stomach that came on any time she talked about the wedding was happiness or nerves. Happiness, she told herself firmly.

Luke glanced at the clock on the stove and finished a last swallow of coffee. "I need to head out. Walk with me to the truck for a minute. I want to show you something."

"Sure." Jenny put his dishes in the sink and followed him out.

Luke pulled a gift bag from his truck and handed it to her. Shoving his hand in his pants pockets, he gave a slow smile. "It's October 15th. Happy anniversary of the day we met."

Jenny couldn't believe he'd remembered. Luke was not a flowery, overly romantic guy.

"You are so thoughtful," she said and rummaged through the tissue paper. Pulling out a box, she glanced at him nervously, hoping it wasn't jewelry. She wasn't a jewelry kind of girl. Her new ring worried her enough. If it was a nice necklace or bracelet, she'd break it or lose it within days. Pulling off the lid, she broke into a relieved smile as she pulled out her gift, a red foam doodad. Turning it over in her hands, she tried to figure out what it was.

"It's a floating key ring." Luke looked proud of himself. "If you drop your boat key ring in the lake, you won't lose it."

"How smart," Jenny murmured and reached up to kiss him, deciding she could work with him on his skills in non-jewelry gift giving. Ashe had given Charlotte a carpet steamer for Christmas, but with her tutelage, had gifted her a day spa package for her birthday. Men *could* be trained.

"There's more." Luke pointed at the truck bed.

Jenny hid a smile. Maybe he'd bought her a bag of miracle growth composted cow manure or a replacement for the tricky garbage disposal in her kitchen.

Luke easily lifted a ten-foot-tall sapling from the truck and thunked the root ball on the ground. "It's a pink dogwood, your favorite. Thought we could plant it and enjoy it as we spend happy years together." His ears turned red, the way they did when he felt strong emotion.

Jenny felt a wave of love as she stepped into his arms. "You are the sweetest man, Luke."

After Luke left, Jenny floated around on a wave of contentedness as she finished tidying the kitchen. The man needed no tutelage in the gift-giving department after all.

In her eyes, that pink dogwood was the most romantic gift she'd ever been given.

CHAPTER 2

OR THE NEXT FEW DAYS, Jenny and Landis worked companionably together on chores. The man her mother had married didn't talk much while he worked, but he was amiable and knew a lot, and those qualities went a long way in Jenny's book. She was still new to cabin ownership, and his matter-of-fact advice and suggestions were helpful. They checked roofs and chimneys; they cleaned gutters. They checked for any cracks in caulking and resealed the ones they found with a special cabin caulk. When the caulk dried, they gently power-washed away any mold and mildew on the cabin exteriors.

As usual, guests were intrigued by the cabins, and Landis patiently answered questions from two husbands who wandered over, asking what they were up to and confessing that they'd always wanted to own a cabin. The Silver Bullet also tended to draw admirers.

When Jenny and Landis finished, they shut off the exterior faucets and stored the hoses.

"Well done, Jenny." Landis gave an approving nod, rocking on his heels as he gave the cabins one last appraising look. "We're all buttoned up for the winter."

"You were a big help," Jenny said gratefully. "I feel like I need to take notes when you talk. I've got a lot to learn about owning cabins and about this resort," she admitted.

"You're getting the hang of it," he said with a reassuring smile. Raising his hand in a wave, the big man whistled tunelessly as he ambled off back to the Redbud, the cabin that he and Jenny's mother were staying in temporarily until construction on their new home was finished.

Chores went so much faster and easier with help, Jenny thought as she walked back to the Dogwood. Initially, she'd held a grudge against Landis because he wasn't her father, but once she'd given him a chance, she'd liked him more and more each day.

Saturday morning dawned as pretty as the meteorologist had predicted. Glancing at the time, Jenny slicked on a coat of pomegranate lip balm, checked her wallet to make sure she had cash, and headed out the door. It would be fun to help Charlotte, and maybe she'd come across a few finds of her own. Since her cabin was so small, Jenny was disciplined about not buying just to buy, but if she found some cool vintage aprons or retro tablecloths, she'd snap them up. Recalling one of her favorite wardrobe pieces ever, the vintage red cowboy boots she'd found at the rummage sale, Jenny felt a buzz of excitement as she strode toward their meeting place. Mama had offered to drive her big SUV in case Charlotte scored any larger treasures.

Powered by a second cup of coffee, Jenny inhaled a big breath of clean, crisp morning air and felt a flutter of excitement about the day ahead as she headed toward the clearing. Passing the green sedan, Jenny noticed her friend had a new bumper sticker that read, *Drive Nice, Darlin'*. Hmm. Jenny liked the sentiment. Charlotte was on an indignant tear lately about rude drivers.

Her mother Claire was about to navigate the tall step up into her and Landis's shiny SUV when she spotted Jenny. Turning toward her, Claire smiled. "Morning, sweetheart. It's a magnificent day."

"Morning, Mama." After a hug, Jenny put her hands on Claire's shoulders and held her away so she could admire today's outfit, a fluttery, flowered midi dress, a soft pink cashmere cardigan, and a white ruffled jean jacket. Her mother's streaky blonde hair was piled into a messy up-do, and she wore dangly earrings. "You look amazing."

"Oh, go on," Mama said, but flushed, looking pleased at the compliment.

Throughout Jenny's childhood, Mama's wardrobe had consisted of baggy slacks and tops in grays and browns. Living with Jax had worn her down. After she'd finally divorced him and married Landis, she'd blossomed. Being adored by her husband, taking better care of herself, and finally pursuing her lifelong passion for art had taken years off Claire.

The two of them climbed into the SUV. Jenny turned to her mother. "How are you all, and what's new?"

"Oh, we're well. Landis got up early and went fishing with two cronies he met getting coffee at Gus's Gas-N-Git." Mama shook her head, smiling. "Those retired men all dress like it's a competition to see who can look shabbiest, but one was a cardiologist and the other was a school principal."

"Good for him for finding new friends." Jenny pulled on her seatbelt. "Did you hear from your contractor?"

"He called last night. After all those delays, the new house will be ready next week. We need to get packing," her mother said in an extra-peppy tone.

"That's great." Though Mama had a smile pasted on her face, her eyes weren't smiling. The Over-55 community she and Landis were moving to was in Asheville, forty-five minutes away. "I read an article about Laurel Vista in *Our State* magazine, and it's supposed to be a wonderful place. I know you're ready to get moved, but I'll sure miss you."

A dark cloud passed over her mother's face. She slipped on her sunglasses. "It's been lovely visiting here, but we need to get settled in our own place and get out of your hair."

"You haven't been in my hair. I've loved having you two here." Jenny felt a wave of sadness at the thought of not being able to walk thirty feet to the Redbud and have a cup of coffee with Mama, share a meal with the two of them or pal around with Landis. Her stepfather liked staying busy. Puttering around the property, he'd repaired sticky doors, took guests on boat rides, helped kids put worms on hooks, and generally acted as the calm and pleasant ambassador for the resort.

Charlotte pulled open the car door and hopped in, bringing a burst of fresh air and the scent of the lemony hand lotion that she liked to use. "Morning, ladies," she said cheerily and settled in her seat, taking a swallow of coffee from her aluminum insulated mug.

"Good morning," Jenny and Mama chorused.

Charlotte wore sensible shoes with extra thick wavy soles that made Jenny's lace-up boots look frivolous, a canvas sun hat with chin ties, and a vest with many pockets like the field guides did in the Orvis catalog. The veteran flea market gal was dressed for the hunt. Charlotte pulled walkie-talkies from pockets and handed one to each of them. "We can use these to stay in contact. If you spot a find, call me STAT."

"I'm not sure if the fire department sale is like some of the big flea markets and antique shows you've been to," Jenny said diplomatically.

"All I know is that when I was at Round Top Antiques Fair in Texas last year, these two-way radios were a life-saver." Charlotte gave her a savvy look. "Better to be overprepared than underprepared."

Curious now, Jenny pushed various buttons on the walkie-talkie to see what they could do. "Testing, testing," she called loudly.

Claire jumped as Jenny's voice blared from the walkie-talkie in her hand. Putting a hand on her throat, she burst out laughing. "You scared me, sweetheart."

"Sorry, Mama." Jenny grinned apologetically. She looked back at Charlotte. "I like your new bumper sticker."

"Thank you. With all the new people moving here, drivers *are* more aggressive. This week, the woman in the car behind me just blared the horn because the light turned green and I didn't speed forward like a shot," Charlotte huffed and held up two fingers. "Two seconds. I was two seconds late pulling forward because I was finishing fluffing my bangs. There's no call for that kind of rudeness."

"I agree," Jenny said, meaning it.

"I do, too," Mama looked both ways and pulled onto

the main road, the big SUV gliding ahead smoothly as she accelerated.

Jenny turned to the back seat, remembering her manners. "Charlotte, thank you for the goose," she said politely, then cracked a smile. "What am I supposed to do with him?"

"Why admire and befriend him, silly," Charlotte said airily and waved her hand. "Oh, and you're welcome. He's precious and you can dress him up. He came with the beret, but I'm not sure it suits him." Charlotte tapped her finger on her mouth. "I call him Garland, but you can change his name it if you'd like."

"He's a cheerful guy, and I like the name. Where do I shop for Garland?" Jenny asked.

"I've seen goose clothes on Etsy and in online home stores like Miles Kimball," Charlotte said. "They have all sorts of outfits. For example, if it rains, you can dress Garland in a yellow slicker and a rain hat like the Gorton's fisherman."

"Ah," Jenny said, smiling. She shot a look at her mother, who was chuckling.

"You gals are fun," Mama announced. "All my girlfriends back home just used to complain about their husbands and talk about their latest medical condition." She gave a little shudder. "Where to find goose clothes is a lot more interesting topic."

"I'm shifting gears here," Jenny announced, feeling the ball of anxiety that had been at the pit of her stomach all week. "It's October 19th already, and I have too many open cabins for the holidays. How can I make this Christmas at the Lakeside Resort even more special? The online reviews from last year were good, but I got a few comments from folks wishing we had more festivities going on. So, I got ahead of myself and mentioned on social media that we had special Christmas surprises planned for guests. Now people are asking what's planned, and I have no idea."

"I'm full of ideas." Charlotte thought about it. "Last year was very special at the resort with the roaring fires, the fantastic tree, and the blizzard. Of course, the impromptu wedding with all the guests invited will be hard to beat. That was over-the-top romantic." She sighed dreamily.

"It *was* romantic." Jenny said, fondly remembering that magical day when Luke's sister Alice had married Mike. "We'll have to come up with another big hit."

Mama pursed her lips. "Fireworks? No, never mind. Too expensive, and it would scare all the animals."

Jenny nibbled a nail. "How about guests go caroling from cabin to cabin?" Squinting, she tried to picture it. "Never mind. Silly idea. There are only eight cabins. While you walked to your neighbor's cabin to sing to them, you'd bump into your neighbor who was heading toward your place to serenade you."

"You're right." Mama drummed her fingers on the steering wheel. "But people do love carols."

Charlotte raised a brow. "What if my design program buddies and I decorate each cabin with a different holiday theme like Santa's Workshop or Polar Express?" Her eyes sparkled with excitement. "We could invite people in town to come take a candlelight tour, like a Christmas Tiny Cabin Tour."

"Good idea but, hopefully, I'll have guests staying in those cabins," Jenny reminded her.

"Hmmm," Mama said. "I have a visualization technique I use when I get stuck and need a creative direction for my painting. First, I close my eyes and breathe deeply."

Jenny shot Charlotte a skeptical look, but her friend's eyes were already closed. Gamely, Jenny shut her eyes and breathed deeply.

"I'm doing this with you but keeping my eyes open," Mama said deadpan, and Jenny laughed. "Let's all of us think back to some of the happiest Christmas and holiday memories we had as a child and decide exactly what made those memories so special."

The three of them were quiet for several long moments. "Okay, girls. Open your eyes. Let's each talk about a favorite memory," Mama said encouragingly.

"One year when I was eight or so, Mama and Daddy took me to the Homestead Resort in Virginia for the holiday and we went on a carriage ride. Even though there was no snow on the ground, the stable hands had dressed up the horses and decorated the wagon to look like

Santa's sleigh. We went on the most fabulous carriage ride. I still get happy when I think of that day," Charlotte said with a sigh.

"Well done, Charlotte." Mama looked over at Jenny. "Do you have yours yet?"

"Not just yet," Jenny said, busily trying to forget what she was currently remembering.

"No hurry, sweetheart," Mama said reassuringly. "I'll go. My happiest memories always involved Christmas music. When I was young, in the weeks leading up to Christmas, my family and I used to always go to church for special choir performances and carol singalongs. It really did help me get in the Christmas spirit." Looking nostalgic, she turned to Jenny. "Did you find your happy memory yet?'

Unfortunately, the only memory Jenny could retrieve was one in which Jax had promised to take her to see Santa at the big, upscale mall in Charlotte, but then left town for a big business opportunity right before they were leaving the house. Jenny vividly recalled wearing a new red plaid Christmas dress and crying hard as a grim-faced Mama explained Daddy's departure. Mama had tried to fix it by taking her to the mall to see the Santa, but Jenny just remembered feeling bereft. Glancing at her mother, who was chuckling at something Charlotte had said, Jenny decided she'd keep that little memory to herself. "I always liked the visits with Santa," she said with forced cheerfulness.

The three of them thought about it.

"We could figure out a way to have a sleigh ride with a wagon. I'll talk to Luke and between his family's farm and all the customers he knows at the hardware store, maybe we could make that happen," Jenny said.

"I love it!" Charlotte clapped her hands in excitement. "We could build a big bonfire afterward and give guests blankets to snuggle under."

Mama looked over at Jenny. "I think you could figure out a way to bring music and Santa to the resort. That nice young woman Lily who stays in the Gardenia might know some resources. As the county librarian, I image she's pretty well connected."

"Great ideas. Okay, sleigh rides, carols, and Santa." Jenny's brain was whirring. "I'd like to invite people from the community to some of the events. They've been so supportive of the resort. This could be our way of thanking them."

"I like those ideas. Now you, or *we*, just need to make it happen," Mama said. "Landis and I will to help any way we can. It'll be fun."

"Count me in, too." Charlotte cleared her throat. "Ahem. Now, I'm shifting gears." With a businesslike look on her face, she pulled a scribbled list from her purse. "Ladies, here is the BOLO list. That's picker talk for items to *be on the lookout for*. I need accent chairs, even if they're ratty. I need lamps, but only if there are two of them. Vintage water skis are hot. Look for lake-related memorabilia, like books or old pictures of families on the water. Dog prints always come in handy. Cool baskets, macramé, bowls, and rugs are useful though I'd need to sniff the rugs before I buy them. I got a beauty at an estate sale last year. When I got it home, I realized it smelled of dog tinkle." She wrinkled her nose. "That smell never comes out. Never."

The parking lot of the fire hall was already packed, even though the sale didn't officially start for another ten minutes. Mama expertly swung the big SUV into the last slot in a line of cars parked on a grassy roadside.

"Are we too close to a ditch bank?" Jenny asked nervously.

"I've got plenty of room," Mama said, a confident look in her eye as she switched off the ignition.

The three of them stepped out of the SUV.

When Jenny paused to adjust her wrinkled sock in her boot, she heard a cry, a muffled thud, and then a small moan. Wildly, she glanced over to the driver's side of the SUV. Mama had disappeared.

Charlotte realized something was wrong at the same moment Jenny did, and they both scrambled around to the other side of the car.

Mama was sprawled in the grassy ditch, groaning and touching her right foot.

"Oh, dear Lord." Charlotte whipped out her phone to dial 911.

Awkwardly, Jenny clambered down the steep slope

into the ditch. Fighting the urge to help Claire stand, Jenny tenderly took her mother's face in her hands. "Mama, are you okay?"

Pale as milk, Mama tried to move her foot and closed her eyes, wincing with pain. In a voice barely above a whisper, she murmured, "I'm fine but believe I've broken my ankle."

CHAPTER 3

WITH JENNY AT THE WHEEL of the Landis's SUV, the two women followed the ambulance to the Emergency Room at First Carolina Regional Hospital. Charlotte called Luke and Ashe to fill them in on what had happened. When Luke offered to meet them at the hospital, Jenny had shaken her head no. "Tell him I think we're going to be okay, but we'll call him if we need him." The last thing she wanted to do was heap more on his already full plate.

While Charlotte did Sudoku on her phone in the waiting room, Jenny sat with Mama in the treatment room. She fretted, knowing how much Landis would want to be here. The calls she'd made to him had gone straight to voice mail. Jenny had texted him, too, and hoped one of her messages would get through.

The orthopedic doctor, a tall, intense-looking young

woman with black-framed glasses, strode into the room so quickly that her white coat flapped behind her. "Good morning. I'm Jane Goodson." She shook Claire's hand and gave Jenny a brief smile. Sliding the films into the X-ray machine, she pursed her lips and looked at Mama. "Mrs. Collins, you've fractured your fibula, the bone of the ankle joint."

"I thought so," Mama said quietly.

Jenny shuddered inwardly. Scooting her chair closer to the bed, she held her mother's hand.

"In the scheme of things, you were very lucky. With a fall like the one you described, you could have easily broken a hip." The doctor pushed her glasses up her nose and went on. "The fracture is stable and occurred in the upper half of the bone. The fracture won't require surgery, but you've also got a sprain, torn ligaments, and bruising to contend with."

Despite the complications, Jenny felt a wave of relief that Mama didn't need surgery.

"We'll start you off with rest, ice, and elevation of the ankle," Dr. Goodson said. "After the swelling subsides, you'll transition to a walking boot. I'm referring you to an orthopedic specialist."

"How long before my mother's ankle is completely healed?" Jenny asked.

Dr. Goodson leveled a gaze at her. "If all goes well, six to eight weeks."

"Oh, dear," Mama said in a reedy voice.

"My nurse will be in to give you instructions, and we'll get you checked out. Best of luck to you, Mrs. Collins." Dr. Goodson hurried off, her lab coat billowing behind her.

Landis whirled into the room, white-faced and grim. Leaning over the bed, he tenderly kissed Claire's cheek. "I'm sorry, love. I was on the boat and had no signal. I got my buddy to drop me off here as soon as I got word." He grimaced. "I'm sorry I wasn't here for you when you needed me."

Jenny quickly filled him in on the diagnosis and treatment plan.

Mama sent him a reassuring smile. "Jenny and Charlotte took good care of me."

Landis sent Jenny a grateful look. "Thank you, Jenny."

"You're welcome."

Landis blew out a ragged sigh of relief. He looked at Claire. "You've got to be bruised and banged up, too." Frowning, his eyes swept over her.

"I will be sore, but the doctor said I'm going to be fine." Claire took one of his hands in hers. "Everything is going be fine, honey."

Landis patted Claire's hand and gave her a smile. "We can handle this, Mama. I'll take good care of you."

Mama smiled beatifically at him. "I know you will." She hesitated and gestured toward her propped-up ankle. "But with this ankle, we can't possibly move to Laurel Vista until much later."

As the nurse entered the room and rattled off discharge instructions to Landis, Jenny looked at her mother curiously. Was it her imagination, or had Mama sounded downright pleased about not being able to move to their new home?

After stopping at the drug store for supplies, Jenny and Charlotte helped Landis get Mama settled in downstairs on the sofa of their cabin. Mama looked wan and tired, and Jenny and Charlotte headed out to give the patient a chance to rest.

Outside, Charlotte got a call from Ashe and paused to give him an update. "Yes, thank goodness. She'll make a full recovery. You, too, boo-boo. You are my sweetums."

Jenny winced as Charlotte made smooching sounds into her cell before she hung up. "I can't decide if you two are sweet or just annoying. I'm going with sweet because I love you," she groused.

Charlotte grinned. "Ashe sends best wishes to Claire for a speedy recovery."

The next day, Jenny made an early morning grocery store run and came home with ingredients for several easy but healthy freeze-ahead casseroles. Landis was a love, but if Mama counted on him for meals, they'd be eating a lot of his favorites, frozen mac and cheese, Hungry Man biscuits, and scrapple. Mama would survive her broken leg but end up back in First Carolina Regional with sudden onset heart disease.

Jenny sighed heavily as she put up groceries and

preheated the oven. She was feeling down and realized she was replaying in her head the scene of Mama lying crumpled in the ditch. Jenny gave herself a mental pep talk. Mama would make a full recovery. She was in good spirits. Everything would be fine. Glancing out the window, she saw the smoke rising from the Redbud, and knew Landis would be treating the patient like a queen.

Feeling marginally better, Jenny changed into soft sweats and her red cowboy boots, footwear that always lifted her mood. Slipping on her favorite vintage apron, a colorful fall number from the fifties with the red and gold falling leaves and orange pumpkins, she sautéed zucchini, spinach, and mushrooms for a vegetable lasagna recipe she'd found in a *Southern Living* magazine.

A text sounded, and Jenny glanced at her phone. The message was from her neighbor, Ella Parr, the bestselling crime novelist.

Ella wrote: *Heard about your mama. Sorry. Dropping by some grub. You home?*

Jenny smiled. News traveled fast in this small community, and she had such kind neighbors. Practical and blunt, Ella's no-nonsense advice about lake living had saved Jenny's bacon time and time again as she grew from a townie to a country woman. Thanks to her friend, Jenny knew not to panic at late spring swarms of damselflies, had a formula to bathe the animals after they'd been skunked, and carried cooler bags and ice packs when she made the summertime trek to the only decent grocery thirty miles away.

Come on by! Jenny tapped out. Pulling from the fridge the ingredients for her next casseroles, Jenny heard a car pull into the gravel driveway and smiled as she swung open the door. "Good morning."

"Morning yourself." Not a touchy feely sort, Ella gave her shoulder a bracing pat. "Sorry about your Mama's tumble. Is she going to be okay?"

"She will," Jenny said firmly, trying to sweep out of her mind the possibility that Mama

would get one of the serious complications that she'd read about on Web MD last night, like nerve injury, infection, or gangrene.

Ella held up a canvas tote. "I made a chicken and corn chowder and lemon bars."

"Yum." Jenny took the bag that was proffered and peered at Ella. Her neighbor looked different. Instead of her blonde-gray Shirley Temple-like curls springing from her head at odd angles, her hair was sleek and pulled back in a floral hairband. Her cream-colored fleece did not have one coffee stain on it, and she did not have on the two strands of reading glasses that she wore when she was in the middle of a book. "You're not writing for a deadline?"

"Nope, I'm taking a break for the holidays. My readers would want a book every month if they could get one, but I need a life." Ella gave a firm nod as if that was that.

"Since Paul finally retired, I'm trying to cut back. Next week, we're taking one of those river cruises in Europe. We'll float around Paris, hit Giverny, check out Rouen, and pay our respects at the Normandy beaches."

"Good for you," Jenny said, meaning it. Ella worked flat out when she was writing and deserved a break. "I want to hear all about that trip. It's on my bucket list."

"Will do." Looking thoughtful, Ella leaned against the kitchen counter. "How's your Mama going to get around while she's recovering? Doctors these days like to keep you moving."

"They do," Jenny said. "Luke and Landis had a long discussion about it last night. They're going to have a walkway built out of composite decking and loop it around the whole property."

"You wanted to make the cabins more disability-friendly anyway, right?"

"Right," Jenny was impressed with Ella's ability to remember something she'd just mentioned in passing almost a year ago. "The walkways will make the lake and the views even more accessible to everybody."

"I like that idea." Ella shot her a questioning look. "You know it's deer season, right?"

Puzzled, Jenny cocked her head at her neighbor. "Okay…"

"If your contractor's a hunter, you won't get your walkway until January."

"Ahhh." Jenny touched the palm of her hand to her

forehead. Would she ever learn the ins and outs of country living?

"One of Paul's old parishioners is a decking contractor who gets to jobs quickly and is reasonable." Whipping a phone from her pocket, she tapped out a text to Jenny. "Tell Luke and Landis to try this fellow."

"You're a lifesaver, Ella," Jenny said. "Any other news from the neighborhood or tips for country living?"

"Tilden Green is the owner of Slowpoke's Diner, that place in Jamison where the food's so good. He's cooking complete takeaway Thanksgiving suppers for folks, birds to pecan pies, and he's not charging an arm and a leg." She waved a hand. "You just pay your money and pick up that whole deal in a cardboard box."

"Brilliant." The food at Slowpoke's was delicious. She'd buy the takeaway meal for herself this year and pull off an easy-peasy spread for Luke and his folks, Landis, and Mama. Her mind raced. She'd recommend the idea to guests arriving at the resort for Thanksgiving and Christmas. Many of them probably wanted a traditional meal on a holiday but didn't want to cook. "Ella, you're a genius."

"I try," Ella said drily and tilted her head. "What kind of shindig are you throwing for your guests this Christmas? I saw on social media that you're planning some razzle-dazzle."

Jenny took an imaginary key and pretended to lock her mouth. "Top secret for now. Really top secret." But she couldn't fib to Ella. "So top secret I don't even know what we're planning. But I will soon, so keep checking back."

Ella chuckled. "I love a good mystery."

"One thing I know. For some of the special events, we're inviting our friends from the community, too, not just guests. So, we want to see you and Paul."

"Count on it. Now, I need to skedaddle. I've got to get us packed." Ella headed toward the door, but paused and looked at Jenny. "Paul would be happy to hold a service for you all on Christmas morning. We'll be in town."

Jenny clasped her hands together, delighted. A service would be a very meaningful missing piece for lots of folks. "I'd love it if he'd do that."

"I'll let him know. Au revoir, mon amie." Ella gathered her empty canvas tote and headed out. "Tell your Mama I'll come see her when I get back, whenever she's ready for company."

On Friday morning, Jenny sat chin in hand, staring at her computer screen. The pre-holiday newsletter she was trying to write was a beast.

Jenny wished she could blame her lack of focus on the sounds of whining power saws and drills from right outside her window, but those sounds didn't bother her a bit. To her, it was the sound of progress. Rufus Butler and his crew were knocking out the whole property walkway. They were meticulous, hard workers who added graceful swooping turns and a few paths to take fanciful side trips to particularly scenic views. Luke and Landis were pleased with the work he and his crew were doing.

For an hour, Jenny had been typing and deleting lame opening lines, *"Fall into Autumn! Here comes Thanksgiving and Christmas!* and *Are you ready for Santa?* Good grief. Where was her creativity? What was she trying to convey?

Helping Landis care for Mama had taken some time, so Jenny still didn't have the specifics of Christmas events, but she wanted to remind people that the holidays were fast approaching, the lake was a picture postcard this time of year, and they needed to hustle and get their reservations made.

Glancing out the window, Jenny saw geese winging by in a V formation and heard their plaintive cries. The leaves on the trees surrounding the lake were brilliant and gray blue clouds scudded across the skies. Jenny sat bolt upright. Pictures. She needed pictures to convey her message.

Grateful Charlotte had popped back by for a day or two, Jenny knocked on the door of the Airstream, hoping her idea had merit. Her friend came to the door wearing her workout clothes, a pink velour sweat suit and a hairband reminiscent of the one Olivia Newton-John wore when she was getting "Physical." Despite her outfit, with her wide-set eyes, black curls, and lush proportions, Charlotte looked gorgeous despite her being convinced she was too fat.

"Hey, there," Charlotte said, panting. "I'm slimming my thighs with my Turbo Barre DVD. Want to join me?"

"Oh, no, thanks," Jenny said hurriedly, almost desperately. The last time she'd tried that grueling class on DVD with Charlotte, she'd limped so badly afterward that people at the resort kept rushing to open doors for her. "Are you up for a boat ride?"

"Always." Charlotte did a deep lunge without the leg trembling and jiggling that Jenny's leg had done the time she did one.

"Come by at 5:45. The leaves are turning, and I need dazzling fall pics for my newsletter. Sunset is 6:26, so we'll get that golden light."

"Sounds fun." Holding the doorframe, Charlotte did an impressive deep plié. "I'll be there with bells on."

Sheesh. Jenny was sore from just watching her.

Later that day, Jenny slipped on a windbreaker and went to the dock to take the cover off the boat and brush away the ever present spider webs. Though the temperature was in the forties, the wind on the lake was chilly. Hands on hips, Jenny spun slowly around, admiring the red, orange, and yellow foliage on the trees along the lake bank. The leaves had already peaked in the higher elevations of the Blue Ridge Parkway, but they were just approaching their peak here. Just right for the shots she needed.

Charlotte did a skipping walk down to the dock and climbed aboard. "I love boat rides." She claimed her seat in the co-captain's chair as Jenny eased the boat from the lift and they glided off. Charlotte stepped up to the helm and idled the boat fifty feet out from the cabins so Jenny could get shots she wanted. The semicircle of cabins with their chocolate brown logs and dark green metal roofs against a clear blue sky was pretty enough. But with the flaming orange maples and bright yellow poplars as a backdrop, Jenny couldn't take a bad shot. With the honey gold sun starting to sink in the sky, the two of them raced across the lake to other scenic spots they'd scoped out: a granite cliff face with a red-leafed dogwood perched atop it, an island that rose out of nowhere, and an old railroad bridge that was a sanctuary for birds.

They headed back. Jenny slowed the boat as they approached the dock and gave Charlotte a thumbs-up. "We got some pretty shots. Thanks, girl."

Her friend returned the thumbs-up. Fiddling with her cell, Charlotte handed it to Jenny and watched her hit the play arrow.

"Wow." Jenny broke into a grin. Charlotte had shot a six-second video clip of Jenny standing at the helm of the pontoon as they raced across the water. In the gold light, Jenny's hair was flying back, the scenery in front of the boat was like a postcard of Maine in the fall, and viewers could hear the thrum of the powerful engine. "Anyone seeing this would feel like they were in a the boat with us on this incredible fall evening."

Charlotte dimpled, took back her phone, and sent Jenny the clip. "Put that baby in your newsletter."

Jenny eased the boat back into the slip without ramming any pilings, and the two made quick work of putting the cover back on.

As they walked up the steps to the resort, Charlotte turned to her. "I'm going to leave tonight and stay at my apartment. I just got a design job back in Shady Grove. Some friends of Mama and Daddy's are downsizing. They're finally ready to put the house on the market and are hiring me to help them go through the house and separate the valuable stuff from the stuff to donate. Then, I'll stage the place and hold an estate sale. Can you believe it?"

"Congratulations, girl. The job sounds like it was made for you," Jenny said, excited for her talented friend.

"I'm tickled to pieces," Charlotte burbled. "Are you still coming into town tomorrow to help me shop for wedding dresses?"

"Tomorrow at 11:00 at the Elegant Bride. I wouldn't miss it."

"Good," Charlotte said as they arrived at Jenny's cabin. "What are your plans for tonight?"

"I'll get this newsletter out. Then, I'm visiting Mama." She raised a brow at Charlotte. "She sounded tickled pink to delay the move to Asheville. If that's so, I want to find out why."

CHAPTER 4

FTER WAVING GOODBYE TO CHARLOTTE as she tootled off in her green sedan, Jenny squared her shoulders and went back inside. No pressure at all, but she needed to write a killer newsletter.

Jenny did fifteen jumping jacks to get the blood going to her brain, shook out her fingers to get them loose and creative, and sat down at the computer. Buddy was under the table napping, so she rested her socked feet on his warm back and gave him a back scratch with her toes. Pulling up her newsletter template, she tried to imagine the dream Christmas she wanted for her guests. After several deep breaths, her fingers flew across the keys.

Warm greetings from your friends at the Lakeside Resort! To remind you of how scenic and peaceful it is here on Heron Lake, have a look at some pictures we took less than an hour ago and several pics from last year's memorable Christmas at the Lakeside Resort.

Jenny set up a slide show featuring the trees with their brightly colored leaves, the exteriors of the cabins, last year's white Christmas, the romantic lakeside wedding, and a few shots of Bear, Buddy, and Levi playing, snoozing, or just looking precious. Those three men were real crowd-pleasers. She tapped on.

Thanksgiving is right around the corner. If you'd like to escape the holiday travel and hustle and bustle, come stay with us at the Lakeside Resort. For those of you who enjoy a traditional meal this time of year but don't feel like cooking, we've worked out an arrangement with a marvelous local restaurant, Slowpoke's Diner, and they will deliver a complete turkey, ham, or vegetarian dinners right to your cabin door! Here are links for details.

To get you in the holiday spirit, during the month of December we have scheduled several festive events for you and your families. We promise you the chance to make memories that last a lifetime... and great photo ops.

Take a Jingle Bells-inspired horse-drawn wagon ride around the property, followed by fireside hot chocolate, s'mores, and spiced cider or mulled wine for the adults! For your kids and grands, we have a very special treat! The Big Man himself, Santa

Claus, has set up a satellite workshop here at Heron Lake, and your young ones will have the chance to visit with him and give him their Christmas lists! For those of you who love Christmas music, we have glorious evenings of performances by choirs and choral groups and we'll do some caroling.

Remember, whether you celebrate Christmas, Hanukah, Kwanza, or are spiritual but not religious, you are always most welcome at the Lakeside Resort. Our guests may participate in any activities or none of them. Many folks are very happy spending cozy evenings fireside in their rustic cabins, reading good books or playing board games. For the outdoors lovers, you might take a winter hike in nearby Heron Heights Park, bird-watch, or bring your bikes and enjoy riding the twenty-six miles of trails.

We'd love to see you. Cabins are filling up fast, so go ahead and make your reservations. Here's a six-second video to remind you of how truly lovely it is here at Heron Lake.

Jenny attached the clip of that boat ride. If this newsletter didn't get the Welcome Inn reservation system humming and the phone lines ringing, she'd eat her hat.

After she ran spellcheck and read it aloud twice to double-check herself, Jenny hit the SEND button. Sitting back in the chair, she took a moment to let herself feel good about the holiday she'd just described. Closing her laptop, Jenny raked fingers through her hair and smiled ruefully as she rose. Now, she just needed to do the hundred things that needed to be done to make it all happen

Jenny slipped on a fleece jacket and headed across the clearing to the Redbud, determined to find out what was on Mama's mind.

When she yoo-hooed and knocked, Landis opened the door and gave Jenny a toothy smile. He patted her so heartily on the back that she coughed a little. "Hey there, Jenny."

"Hey there, yourself." Jenny quietly asked, "How's Mama?"

Landis rubbed his balding pate, looking pleased. "She'd doing great. We took a little stroll this morning. She's doing her exercises and says she's not too uncomfortable."

Mama lounged on the sofa, pillows surrounding her and her foot propped up. Beaming, she waved Jenny over. "Hey, there, honeybun. Come see me."

Kissing her cheek, Jenny pulled a chair up and sat beside her. "You look good, Mama."

"I feel pretty good, too. My ankle is coming along nicely, though I may have overdone it today." Claire pushed back a lock of hair that had fallen in her face. "Love the new walkway the men are building. With the one long loop done, it makes it so much easier to get my exercises done."

Landis poked at the fire in the robin's egg blue wood-stove and looked at Jenny. "If you'll keep your mama company, I'll restock that woodpile. We're running low on logs."

"Sure." Jenny reached over to hold her mother's hand as Landis shrugged on a jacket, grabbed a canvas log carrier, and headed out the door.

"How are you doing with not being able to get around as easily as before?" Jenny knew how much Claire liked to stay on the go.

Mama made a face. "It's tricky. I can get around, but it still hurts some and everything takes longer. Landis has to help me with my shower and getting dressed, but he's been such a lamb about it."

Jenny nodded. "So you're putting weight on the foot?"

"Slowly but surely, thank heavens." Looking away for a moment, Mama smoothed a wrinkle from her blanket. "I'll be right as rain before you know it, but I still think it'd be best to put off our move."

There was the disconnect again. Though Mama sounded disappointed, she looked relieved. Jenny would test her theory. "Mama, there's no need to delay your move. Luke, Charlotte, and I could get you settled at the new house. We could help Landis get y'all unpacked and organized."

Claire's eyes widened. "Oh, no, honey. We couldn't possibly impose," she said hurriedly.

Jenny wasn't sure whether to say anything or not, but after their period of estrangement, she and her mother had vowed to always be truthful with one another. "Mama, you don't seem excited about moving. Is there anything going on that I should know about?"

Mama put a hand to her mouth and suddenly blinked back tears. "I don't want to leave," she said in a strangled tone.

Whoa. "I would think being nervous about a move is natural," Jenny said tentatively.

Now Mama began crying in earnest. Reaching for a tissue, she dabbed at her eyes. "Our old house in Summerville was 5,000 square feet. Five thousand." She threw up her hands. "While Landis worked, I only saw him after very long days at the bank, and he was tired. When he retired, all he did was play golf and watch his stocks. We could go days without really talking to each other." She shook her head. "Our time here in this darling little cabin has been the happiest we've ever had. The new house in Laurel Vista is 3,500 square feet. Still too big by far. This is all we need." She circled a finger around the small cabin she and Landis had called home for the past four months. "We've gotten to be even better friends here. Funny thing to say about someone you've been married to for so long, but it's true." In a quavering voice, she blurted out, "I wish we never had to leave."

Jenny found herself gaping and made herself stop. "I didn't know you felt this way, Mama."

"It's true." Mama grabbed another tissue, blotted her tears, and tried to collect herself.

"Does Landis know how you feel?" Jenny asked quietly.

Her eyes filling again, Mama shook her head no. "He might suspect, but we've never talked about it." Her mother wasn't finished talking. "Another thing. Laurel Vista is kind of fancy." She grimaced. "I am so *over* fancy. I love the wildness and the beauty of this place." Her hand on her heart, Claire gestured toward the window. "That view of Heron Lake is the prettiest thing I have ever laid eyes on. So serene and ever-changing. It just makes me want to paint and paint and paint." She threw up her hands and looked resigned. "But I can't ask you to let us stay on, honey. You've already been so good to us."

Jenny's mind raced as she considered how she felt about the prospect of Mama and Landis living at the Lakeside Resort. She'd had qualms about it when they'd first come to stay, mainly because she'd never gotten to know Landis, and childishly, she'd resented him for taking her Daddy's place. But Daddy had been long gone when Landis met Mama. Jenny had come to know her stepfather better and grown to love him. But what if the arrangement was permanent? How did she feel about that? How would *Luke* feel about that? Reaching over, Jenny squeezed her mother's hand. "Before we decide on anything, you need to let Landis know your thoughts, and I need to talk with Luke about it. Let's each do that, and then talk."

"Are you sure I'm not asking too much to even have you consider it?" Mama asked in a shaky voice, doubt in her eyes.

"You're not. Let's just talk to the men and think it over." Jenny tried to keep her features neutral. After she went bridal dress shopping with Charlotte tomorrow, she could stop in to see Luke at the store and broach the subject with him. He was coming for supper Sunday night, so they could hash it out more if need be. Luke was brave enough to take her on, but how would he feel about living within stone's throw of his in-laws?

Before the sun rose the next morning, Jenny was at the computer. The reservations were coming in fast and furious. Her picturesque newsletter had done the trick. She felt a fizzy happiness in her chest, but she needed to get the entertainment arranged fast.

Right around Christmas, she now had more requests for reservations than she had available cabins. If she got those exciting holiday activities planned during other weekends in December, she might be able to persuade guests to consider dates other than the weekend of December 20th.

Jenny pinched her lip and thought about it. Lily, her librarian tenant, was moving out soon, so now the Gardenia would be available to rent, too. She did the math in her head. Lily had been a long-term tenant when

Jenny had desperately needed the stable income. She'd charged the young woman a lower rate than she now knew she could get for nightly, weekend, and weekly cabin rentals. One more cabin available to rent at a higher price solved one problem.

Jenny mulled it over. If she camped out in the Silver Bullet, she could rent the Dogwood, too. She shuddered inwardly. She didn't like doing that. Jenny had done it before when she'd had a full house, but having to clear out all of her personal stuff was a chore, and she didn't like to think about guests sleeping in her bed and poking around in her personal space. Grudgingly, she reminded herself that heavy bookings were another reason for Luke and her having their very own separate cabin. She'd never have to rent out her own private quarters again.

So, she had seven cabins available for rent at the higher holiday rate. If she could book them all almost solidly during the winter high season, she could cruise into the first quarter of 2020 with enough financial cushion that she wouldn't feel so anxious during the hard-to-rent winter months.

Luke's future financial contribution to the resort was an unknown, too. The two hadn't even talked about how they were going to handle money when they married. Would they commingle funds or keep their money separate? Though she knew Luke was financially comfortable with the sale of his part of a business, she didn't know how comfortable. That was another important discussion they needed to have. All Jenny knew was that she was determined to pull her own weight. She needed to make a real go of the resort year round and wouldn't let Luke bail her out.

As she closed out of Welcome Inn, Jenny felt a surge of determination. Rolling her shoulders to get the knots out, she poured herself a tall glass of iced coffee. She needed to hit Christmas planning hard and get those arrangements made.

On the toolbar, she typed in *Rental Santa Claus North Carolina* and got several hits that looked promising. Sitting up straighter in her chair, she found websites and scribbled a list of names and telephone numbers on a pad of paper. At 9:00 AM, she started making her calls.

The first Santa answered the phone with a booming voice. "This is Odell Fox, aka Santa

Claus."

"Good morning. My name is Jenny Beckett, and I own a small resort on Heron Lake. I was wondering if you have any availability to do a Meet Santa event for us during any of the first four weekends in December?"

"Ho, ho, ho," Odell-slash-Santa said with a jolly laugh. "Little lady, I've been booked up since January of last year, and I expect you'll find any of the good rental Santas are all booked up too."

Smarting from the ho, ho, ho-ing at her expense, Jenny stiffly thanked him, hung up, and called a few more rental Santas. As Odell had predicted, three were already booked. One from Charlotte told her he'd have to charge her ten dollars a mile for his *sleigh and reindeer* to travel any more than twenty miles from his home. The last Santa was available, but slurred his words and sounded tipsy. A drunk Santa was the last thing she needed. Hastily, Jenny ended the call.

Jenny scrubbed her face with her hands. Snap. She was spinning her wheels with Santa. Luke had offered to search for horses and a wagon for their sleigh rides. She'd follow up with him. Hopefully, he was having more luck than she was.

Seeing the time, Jenny hurriedly slipped into a go-to-town outfit of khaki slacks, a cream-colored cashmere turtleneck, and a lightweight houndstooth check jacket Charlotte had found for her at a Junior League thrift store in Charlotte. Slicking on claret-colored lipstick, Jenny tossed treats to the dogs, gave Levi a few carrots and headed to Shady Grove.

"So, we're going to find you a fairytale wedding dress." Jenny took a first sip of her delicious caffè mocha. The two of them had stopped in at Jacked-Up Coffee before heading over to the Elegant Bride dress shop.

"Hopefully. I probably should get something simple." Charlotte gave a wry smile as she carefully sipped her frothy latte. "I thought a city hall wedding would be practical, Ashe wanted a big church wedding, and we made a compromise of a medium-sized church. He knows so many people from Celeste that he wants to invite a hundred and seventy-five guests. I think that's too big, but that's what he seems to want." Her friend poured a packet of sugar in her drink and stirred it. "Even though I kept pushing for city hall, I love poufy dresses but the idea of a fancy wedding gown is silly. This is not my first trip down the aisle, although there were technically no aisles at my first wedding, which was in the living room of the Justice of the Peace's ranch house. His wife did throw artificial rose petals, though." She gave a puckish grin. "You may recall that Daddy had…strong opinions about the first groom I picked."

Jenny smiled, remembering. Charlotte's father Beau had been incensed when he'd found out that his unemployed artist son-in-law was helping himself to a lot of Charlotte's money and was trying to convince her to fund a six-month-long painting tour of Europe for him. Beau had had a heart-to-heart talk with his daughter, run off the artist, and helped Charlotte file for divorce. Jenny unwrapped a still-warm pumpkin muffin topped with crumbly cinnamon streusel and took a bite. Delicious. Her own first husband had turned out to be a work-obsessed man who'd had an affair with his boss, and her former fiancé Douglas was now living with a much-younger physical therapist. "We both had a starter husband," she said firmly.

"I know that's true, but I still wish Ashe was going to

be my first and only husband," Charlotte said wistfully. She dunked a biscotti into her coffee drink and crunched into it.

"I agree." Jenny thought about it. "Getting married again at this age is different, that's for sure. We've lived our lives. We've had heartaches and losses and know marriage is more than a pretty ceremony." She took a sip of coffee. "It's because we're wiser that we found such good men. Ashe adores you. You finally got the real deal and should celebrate it any way you want to." She tapped a finger on the table to emphasize her point. "If you want city hall, work on Ashe. If you want a big, poufy wedding dress and ten bridesmaids, you should have that."

"You're right." Charlotte pointed at her with her wooden coffee stirrer. "I'm going to give you this same lecture when you start planning your wedding."

Jenny broke into a grin. "Fair enough. Let's go look at wedding dresses."

At the Elegant Bride, Jenny sat on a white velvet couch holding a chilled glass of Prosecco in her hand as Eugenia, the proprietress with the blonde bob so smooth that it looked shellacked, selected several dresses for Charlotte. "So many of our brides are size two or four. You are *so* lucky that we just got these gowns in for plus-sized gals," the blonde said in a drawl so sweet it set Jenny's teeth on edge.

While Charlotte changed, Jenny eyed Eugenia. She was a woman in her late fifties who'd probably kept her figure by eating only lettuce and secretly smoking cigarettes. Cosmetic procedures must be what made her skin so taut. You could bounce a quarter off her cheeks, and her lips were as plump as the trout Jenny had accidentally caught this summer. Jenny didn't like her.

Charlotte let Eugenia in the dressing room to size up fit, and the comments the proprietress was making made Jenny's blood pressure soar. *"We need a laced-up bodice to contain your girth. That neckline will draw the eye up instead of highlighting your chubbiness."* And, after a big aggrieved sigh, *"Oh, dear. We'll have to let out even these bigger dresses for you."*

Jenny put down her glass of sparkling wine without taking the first sip and felt blood thrum between her ears, noticing that Charlotte's tone had gone from excited to apologetic to subdued. This was the not-so-subtle meanness that Charlotte told her plus-sized women dealt with regularly. Now that Jenny could recognize fat-shaming when she heard it, it just steamed her grits.

After Eugenia bustled out with the last gown in her arms, her mouth quirked in disapproval, Jenny marched over to the dressing room where a dejected-looking Charlotte was slipping on her clothes. "Let's go, girl. You are not buying a thing here. That woman is a witch."

Sensing trouble, Eugenia hurried over, a simpering smile on her face. "So, shall we wrap up the size fourteen for you, or would you like to try on the sixteen just in case you eat seconds on dessert and gain a little weight in your tummy between now and then, Charlene?"

Her face now ashen, Charlotte lowered her eyes, not saying a word.

But Jenny had had enough and stared at the woman, dagger-eyed. "My friend's name is Charlotte, not Charlene," she said crisply.

The woman's eyes flashed in annoyance. "Okay."

Jenny smiled sweetly and pointed at the proprietress. "Eugenia, I'm sure this is not your intention, but you are acting mean to a customer about her weight. Worse, you are taking away my beautiful friend's pleasure at picking out her wedding gown. Not all brides are size two, and not all skinny women are pretty, either inside or out." She let her eyes travel up and down the woman's scrawny frame dismissively. "I own the Lakeside Resort, and we're hosting more and more weddings every day. I can't in good conscience recommend the Elegant Bride to my brides-to-be, and that's too bad, because I like people to shop local. We'll take our business elsewhere." Linking Charlotte's arm in hers, she marched her out the door.

CHAPTER 5

OUTSIDE, CHARLOTTE GAVE HER A grateful smile, tears brimming. "You were amazing. That woman *was* being mean, and you called her on it." She threw her arms around Jenny and then pulled back to give her a puckish grin. "How many weddings have you hosted at the resort?"

"Just the one," Jenny said airily. "But I could have a sudden uptick in weddings." She couldn't keep a straight face and burst out laughing. Charlotte guffawed, and the two laughed their way down Market Street.

Charlotte's face grew serious, and she frowned. "I still need a dress. I'm going to look online, but I might ask you to come with me to shop in Charlotte if I can't find one I like."

Jenny bobbed her head. "Just send me the links to any

dress you want me to see, and of course I'll go with you to shop in Charlotte."

"Thanks, girl." At the corner, Charlotte gave her another hug. "I'm off to see my new clients. I'll see you soon, though. You were wonderful, girly girl." She gave Jenny a kiss on the cheek and strode on, a pep in her step.

As Jenny walked up the block to Main Street where Frank's Friendly Hardware store was located, she thought about how tired Luke had been looking. Hopefully, when he finished training the new manager, Tom, he could rest up and everyone could get back to their lives. She and Luke could enjoy being in love and building a happy future for themselves at the Lakeside Resort. She couldn't wait.

Slowing, Jenny fished her phone from her purse and called Luke. "Hey, there. I'm a little bit early. Do you still have a few minutes for me to visit with you?"

"Always. Come on over," Luke said, not hiding the pleasure in his voice.

Hoo boy. Jenny straightened her spine and headed toward the store. Luke might not be quite so chipper when she asked him about in-laws living right next door.

As Jenny approached the storefront, she saw the decorated display windows and had to smile. As was the norm for Frank's Friendly, after October 1st, ghosts and goblins haunted the first store display window, pilgrims and Native Americans solemnly celebrated the first Thanksgiving in the second window, and a life-sized

Santa boogied to *Rockin' Around the Christmas Tree* in the third. Jenny smiled affectionately. The Hammonds rushed the season and went overboard decorating for every holiday because the women in the family loved it. Jenny pushed open the door, hearing the jingling bell that announced new visitors. The store was as tidy and welcoming as it had been the first time she'd walked in the door just over a year ago and met Luke. She felt a pleasant wave of nostalgia.

A bright-eyed young man in blue hipster glasses who had to be Tom seemed sincerely interested as he helped a customer find just the right paint color, while another part-time employee, college freshman Travis, helped a man buying pipe for a plumbing project.

Tom paused and gave Jenny a friendly smile. "We'll be right with you, ma'am."

Jenny gave a little wave and pretended to examine a rack of American flags. Good manners. Friendly. Intelligent sounding. The young man seemed like a great fit for the position of manager. Jenny crossed her fingers that this one worked out, kept away from online dating websites, and stayed at Frank's Friendly forever.

Luke approached and gave her a peck on the cheek. "Hey, there."

"Hey, yourself." Jenny's breath caught like it sometimes did when he looked at her.

Luke beckoned her. "Let's go out back. I've had a break area built out there."

Travis saw Jenny and waved, and Tom's eyes lit up as he now recognized her as Luke's fiancée. It felt good to be the boss's wife, or almost the boss's wife.

As Luke pushed open the back door, Jenny's eyes widened. What she remembered as a patchy stand of grass with two rickety plastic lawn chairs was now a little oasis. A navy blue resin picnic table stood on a stand of lush grass. Chickadees and sparrows were lunching at a birdfeeder at the back of the small lot, and two old but sturdy-looking wooden lawn chairs painted the same navy blue as the picnic table stood under a tulip poplar with golden orange leaves. "Wow. Just wow," she said. "You've made this area so pretty."

Luke grinned and raised a shoulder. "I'm working on keeping employees. Thought I'd give them a cool break area."

"Great idea." Jenny paused a beat and tilted her head at him. "So Tom's a good guy, and he's not married?"

Luke threw up his hands, feigning exasperation. "No, Jenny. You can't have Tom. You're engaged to *me*."

She swatted him on the arm. "If he fell in love with a nice local gal, voila, they'd both be committed to the area, no more manager turnover, and we'd all live happily ever after."

Luke rolled his eyes, swung a long leg over the seat of the picnic table and sat. "What's new?"

"So much, but I know you're busy. Here's the main thing I wanted to run by you." Jenny sat beside him and took his hand. "I have...some news on the home front. I'm not sure how you're going to take it, but please don't be afraid to say no." Jenny shared the story about Mama's wanting to stay at the Lakeside Resort.

Luke shook his head and whistled. "Whoa. Big news."

Was he upset that she even asked? Jenny tried to read his expression, but Luke just looked...well, like Luke. Amiable, calm, nonjudgmental. His steadiness was part of what she loved about him, but sometimes it drove her mad. "So, what do you think about Mama and Landis being our neighbors? Can you picture us being happy living so close to the two of them?"

Luke paused for a few seconds, looking thoughtful. "I kind of like the idea. I love your Mama and Landis is a stand-up guy. He's easygoing, and he's taken better care of the place than I've been able to since Daddy got sick."

Jenny blew out a breath she didn't know she'd been holding and kissed his cheek hard. Giddily happy, her words came out in a rush. "I'm so glad you feel that way. I've loved having them around. Besides you, now I have other family close to me. Landis and I are buddies. Mama and I are close as can be without either of us butting into each other's lives." Jenny paused to take a breath. "And we can help out when they get older and need us more."

"Don't forget how much they've helped us out too," Luke reminded her. "All the help with guests and upkeep, and Landis has asked me if they can please take care of the resort when we go on our honeymoon." He gave her a meaningful look. "Whenever that is, and wherever it is that we are going."

Jenny flushed, feeling guilty. "I just haven't had a chance to come up with a list of possibilities, but I will soon," she promised.

"I know you will," Luke said.

"Are we still on for supper tomorrow night? I've missed you." Such a good man, she thought, gazing at him fondly.

"Sure. Tell you what, I'll make it easy and pick up a pizza," Luke said.

"After we eat, we can go visit Mama and Landis and tell them that we're happy to have them stay." Jenny felt a buzzy excitement about sharing that news with them.

Luke lifted a brow. "Wonder how Landis is taking hearing your mama doesn't want to move into their new home?"

"I don't know. One thing is for sure. Landis is committed to Mama being happy."

"They'll work it out." Luke assured her with a half-smile. "Tomorrow, I'll show you the cabin plans I've been looking at online. Some are good-looking and could give us just the space we need." He gave her a level look. "We also need to start making plans for our wedding," he reminded her. "When are we getting hitched? Are we getting married on the property, or do we want to pick another venue? We need to make some decisions."

"Great." Jenny tried to sound enthusiastic, but felt disinterested. Odd.

Luke glanced at his watch and gave her an apologetic look. "I need to get back to work. I promised Tom I'd go over accounts receivable with him during the late- morning lull."

"Sure." Jenny leaned toward Luke and gave him a kiss, still floating on air that he'd agreed to let Mama and Landis stay. "Love you, Luke. See you tomorrow."

"Love you, Jenny girl." Luke gave her that dark-eyed, intense look that was meant only for her. Melting a little at his effect on her, Jenny headed for the car.

Back home, Jenny took the animals outside to run around. Afterward, she gathered supplies from the laundry room, cleaned three guest cabins, and ran a big load of sheets. The whole while, a thought niggled at her. She was dreading looking at cabin plans with Luke tomorrow night.

When she'd folded the clothes from the dryer, Jenny fixed herself a cup of peppermint tea and sat at the kitchen table, enjoying the break. Leaning back in her chair, she looked around the Dogwood. She loved every inch of her cabin, the cocoa-brown sturdy logs, the windows that brought the outside in, and the wide-open view of the lake she loved. Since the cabins sat on a bluff, a breeze was always blowing.

Lacing her fingers together and resting them on her stomach, Jenny tipped back the kitchen chair on two legs and looked up to the loft. Her pretty white iron queen bed was there, along with the bird's-eye maple dresser that Mama had inherited from her mama.

Her cheerful living room held the robin's-egg blue, cast-iron wood stove on the raised stone-work slab, the ruby-red leather wingchair her father had given her as a birthday present, and Jax's primitive pine bookcase that still held some of his books and business magazines.

Over the mantle hung Daddy's colorful and detailed hand-drawn rendering of his vision for the Lakeside Resort, including the vintage RVs, the eight tiny cabins in a semicircle facing Heron Lake, red canoes pulled up on the lawn, a rope swing hanging over the water, and a power boat zooming by towing children on tubes. Luke had had Jax's drawing made into a canvas print for Jenny, and it was a gift she treasured.

Thunking the chair back down on all four legs, Jenny shook her head as if to clear it. Maybe she didn't want to move because she just felt sentimental. The furnishings she loved were just *things*, things she could take along with her to the new cabin.

The next evening, Luke arrived at her door with a laptop bag slung over his shoulder and two small pizza boxes in his hand. The spicy aroma of cooked peppers, onions, and zesty pepperonis filled the air, and Jenny's stomach growled loudly. Hoping Luke hadn't heard the unladylike rumble, Jenny popped the pizzas in the oven to warm and opened two frosty bottles of beer.

Luke got settled at the kitchen table, wearing reading glasses that Jenny thought made him look like a hot tamale college professor. Opening the laptop, he found the detailed renderings of four cabins that he thought might suit them best. Jenny laid out paper plates and napkins and served them each slices of their favorites. Luke took a large bite of his pepperoni pizza, and Jenny bit into the warm, cheesy crust with the layers of artichoke, tomato, red pepper, and mushroom. Ah, deliciousness.

"Before we look at details, let me just tell why I thought these might be our top four contenders." Luke pulled a small notebook and pen from his front shirt pocket, flipped it open, and read his notes. "Thought it'd be best to pick a cabin that would sit on the lot to maximize lake views and catch the best sunrises and sunsets. We want it to look similar enough to the existing cabins that it doesn't stick out. Wraparound porches are a must. I think we should buy a package for the cabin and have their crew assemble it for us. Even though I'm a general contractor, I've never worked with logs. Let's pay the pros to do what they do best." Luke looked at her for confirmation and when she nodded, he went on. "Size wise, twenty-four hundred to twenty-eight hundred square feet might work best for us."

"Twenty-eight hundred seems huge for the two of us." Jenny rubbed her temples with her fingers. A headache was brewing. "Are you sure we need to move, Luke?" she asked plaintively.

Luke carefully took off his glasses and rested them on the table. "Practically speaking, I'm not sure I could live with you, all the boys, and my stuff in this cabin." With a thumbnail, he scraped at the label on his beer bottle and sent her a speculative look. "Anything else going on, Jenny? Is there any reason you can think of for us to not build a home that would work best for the future?"

Jenny flushed guiltily as she thought about all the hours he'd spent researching log cabin companies and plans, asking her about preferences, and coming up with budgets and timelines. Leaning toward him, she spoke earnestly. "You're right, Luke. We need to make this move. I'm sorry for being so wishy-washy. Maybe I'm just attached to the cabin because it used to be Daddy's."

Luke nodded his understanding but looked directly at her and held her gaze. "Is there anything else bothering you, Jenny? I know you've had a lot going on, but you've seemed reluctant to plan the wedding, decide on a honeymoon, or get interested in designing our new home." He raised a brow. "Are you still all in on this new life, Jenny girl, or are you getting cold feet?"

Jenny felt her eyes prick with tears and stared at him, suddenly terrified that he might be calling off the wedding. "I'm all in, Luke. I think I'm just having a case of pre-wedding jitters. I'll get over it, I promise." Leaning toward him, she kissed him thoroughly, finally pulling away with a shaky sigh.

He gave her a crooked smile. "If you ever want to talk through those jitters, I'm here for you."

Jenny nodded mutely. She felt vulnerable, not a feeling she liked. "Okay. Now, can we please look at some more cabins?"

Luke turned back to the laptop. Jenny slid her chair closer to his, took a long fortifying slug of beer, and peered at the images he'd pulled up on the screen. Luke took a swallow of his beer, then clicked on an image of their four choices arranged close to each other in a rectangle and looked at her questioningly. "Any you can rule out from just the exterior?"

Jenny tilted her head and studied each more closely. "Not really. They're all good-looking."

"I agree," Luke said, looking pleased. "Each has clean lines. The facades are all balanced and the design is handsome."

"They look welcoming," Jenny said tentatively, hoping she didn't sound fatuous.

"Exactly." Luke beamed at her like she was a star student.

Inordinately proud of herself, Jenny got up to serve them more pizza.

"Let's go through these one by one." Luke opened the drawings and 3-D floor plan for the Aspen, the Ridgeline, the Fancy Gap, and the Blue Ridge.

But Jenny just couldn't focus, her head swimming as she tried to keep track of features she liked and didn't in each. She kept getting the Ridgeline mixed up with the Aspen and thinking the Blue Ridge was the Fancy Gap. After the third time Luke had patiently reminded her about which cabin was which, Jenny rubbed her eyes. "Luke, I'm just too tired to focus on this right now. I like the four you've narrowed it down to, but can we choose later?"

Luke tried to hide the disappointment in his eyes. "I was hoping this might even be fun, but we'll come back to it." Closing the laptop, Luke stood, pulled Jenny to her feet and just held her. "Remember, Jen, if something's bothering you, talk to me about it. I'm not the best communicator anyway, and I can guarantee you I can't read minds."

Jenny just hugged him tighter. She'd tell him what was wrong if she knew what was wrong. Attributing it to pre-wedding jitters didn't seem completely accurate to her, but she was darned if she knew what was going on. She was being a bad bride-to-be and a brat for turning up her nose at these sharp and pretty cabins Luke was offering her. What was wrong with her?

Could her reticence about moving forward be like the feelings Charlotte was having about her wedding? Maybe her disappointments about love made her wonder if she was deserving of a guy as stellar as Luke. Could fears about trusting again be making it hard for her to get gung-ho about plans for the future? She needed to think about it.

Resting her forehead against Luke's, Jenny sighed as she let herself lean into his comforting bulk. One thing she knew was fact. Luke was the big, wondrous love of her life. Jenny would live in a yurt and marry him while skydiving if that's what he wanted to do. She just needed more time.

CHAPTER 6

AFTER THEY TIDIED UP THE kitchen, Jenny and Luke knocked on the door of the Redbud. Landis opened the door beaming and gave them each a hearty pat on the arm. From her bed on the couch, Mama called, "Hello, darlings."

They pulled up chairs around the bed, and Landis poured four mugs of decaf. They all sipped their coffee. Landis cleared his throat. "Your Mama just threw me quite a curveball. I didn't know how strongly she felt about staying here rather than moving."

Claire took Landis's hand. "I didn't know either until it was time for us to move," she said looking sheepish.

"So where do you all stand on this proposition?" Landis asked Jenny and Luke, sounding like the astute businessman he'd been. "This is a mighty big favor we're asking, and we won't think of pursuing it if it doesn't sit well with you."

Claire smiled shakily at them and shredded a Kleenex. "Please be honest with us."

Hiding her smile, Jenny glanced at Luke. "You tell them."

Gravely, Luke looked at Claire and then at Landis. "Jenny and I have talked it over, and we'd be happy for you all to stay on at the resort."

Beaming, Landis heartily clapped Luke on the back and bussed Jenny's cheek.

"Bless your hearts." Claire burst into noisy, happy tears. Jenny rose and hugged her mother, handing her the box of tissues. "Shhh, Mama. This is all going to work out fine."

Mama's tears slowed, and she began to talk as though her words had been pent up. "Here's another thing I didn't like about Laurel Vista. It was manicured and safe just like our house in Summerville was. But I want something different, something wilder, where I can have new adventures. I want to start painting classes here. I want to plant a fragrance garden and grow all sort of flowers for cutting. I want to go to church fish fries and start hiking. I want Landis to teach me to drive the boat."

Landis widened his eyes, pretending to look terrified, and they all chuckled.

Claire pointed a finger at her husband. "You've been happier here too. You've built that crazy meadow and woods golf course and play it with clubs you got at a yard sale. All the men guests flock to you. You've helped Jenny out with the boat and started that vegetable garden. You're much more fun than you were back home."

Chuckling, Landis grinned. "She's right. I'm having a ball."

"I think of you as the head of the welcoming committee." Jenny hooked a thumb at Luke. "He calls you the mayor of the Lakeside Resort."

They all chuckled, but then Luke's face grew serious. "So what are you going to do about your house in Asheville?"

Landis shrugged and held his hands palms up. "We'll sell it. We'll likely lose money, but I don't care. Life's too short to not be doing what you want to do." He gave Claire a look of unabashed love. "And you know what they say. If mama's not happy, nobody's happy."

Jenny sent Luke a twinkling look, and he gave an exaggerated nod of agreement.

The four of them talked, and Luke got on Landis's laptop to pull up the cabins they were considering. The two men leaned forward studying the plans and talking enthusiastically, Luke gesturing toward the screen at certain features. Jenny stayed in her chair, though, talking with her mother. Picking up Claire's treatment summary, she read and reread it as if it were engrossing.

"A bigger cabin might work nicely for you," Claire said, eyeing Jenny.

"Oh, it might," Jenny said breezily.

Mama just gave her a knowing look.

As Jenny put the last of the dishes in the dishwasher, she glanced at her mother and then at the men. "I need all y'all's help with Christmas at the resort."

The men's eyes lit up at the challenge, and Jenny talked about the holes in her big plans.

"I can't find a wagon and horses," Luke said.

"I met a fellow at Gus's whose son has horses." Landis scratched his head thoughtfully. "I'll talk to him about the whole horse-drawn wagon deal."

Luke nodded. "I'll work on Santa. I'll call my brother-in-law. He knows everybody and might be able to help find someone."

Jenny gave them each a look. "Unless y'all come up with a Santa, one of you two men will need to step up to the plate." She hesitated. "But you both are going to be so busy. I'll need you. It'd be best if we could find somebody else to play that part."

"Where are we going to put Santa when he comes to visit the kids?" Mama looked around her living room, which now seemed small with four adults sitting in it chatting.

"The cabins are too small," Luke said. "Plus, they'll all be booked."

"Hmmm. Where to put the big man?" Landis muttered, rubbing his chin.

"We'll figure that out," Jenny said, sounding more

confident than she felt, and glanced at Claire. "Mama, you and I need to come up with ideas about caroling and music." If it was bitterly cold in December, would anyone want to stand outside singing *Jingle Bells*? One more problem with only small cabins. There was no heated gathering area. Maybe a twenty-four-hundred square foot cabin that included a gathering or meeting room *could* make sense.

Luke put a hand on Jenny's shoulder and squeezed it. "Hate to break this party up, but it's getting late." He gave Landis a thumbs-up. "We'll talk."

Jenny leaned in to kiss her mother. "Good night, Mama. Sleep tight and sweet dreams."

Claire's eyes misted as she grabbed Jenny's hand and pulled her closer. "You have no idea how happy you've made me," she said, her voice thick with emotion.

"Love you, Mama." Jenny leaned in for one more kiss. "We're real glad you're staying."

That evening after Luke had left, Jenny wiped down the counters and stove one last time, and got the boys settled in for the evening. Levi was counting sheep in his little cedar mini nest in the corner, and the boys climbed upstairs to the loft with her. It was past 10:30 when Jenny sank into bed, but she found she couldn't sleep.

Beginning with serious global worries, Jenny pictured those poor sea lions in their ocean homes floating among plastic as people gaily tossed away straws and water bottles. She moved to more personal worries. When she was trying to do a million things and drinking large coffees, was the way her heart raced a warning sign of her imminent heart attack? Next, could they could pull off the Christmas they'd promised guests? Online reviews that began with DON'T WASTE YOUR MONEY would be lengthy and scathing. Guests would offer excruciating detail about the poor accommodations and pitiful excuse for holiday entertainment, adding lines like, *Ruined Christmas for my two children* or *My wife just cried with disappointment*.

After tossing and turning with that scenario, Jenny had depressing ruminations about her mother's health, picturing Claire's ankle not healing properly and her having to get a peg leg. Moving on, she pictured their new log cabin, which was now 10,000 square feet. Jenny would be so lonely, reading in her cavernous room, and Luke would be off in another wing. They'd go days without talking, and the marriage would fall apart before their first anniversary.

With a groan, Jenny finally gave up trying to sleep. Pulling off her sleep mask, she turned on the bedside lamp and looked at the small bed space she'd been squashed into by the two dogs. Bear, a notorious bed hog, had spread out perpendicularly across the mattress, and Buddy was lying on Jenny's feet snoring.

Cramped quarters could be part of the reason for her sleeplessness. "Come on, boys. Get in your bed," she called. Both dogs pretended to keep sleeping until she started shoving them off the bed. Sulkily, they hopped down, tried to look pitiful, and moped over to sleep on their orthopedically correct spring-foam dog beds for which Jenny had spent way too much money.

Plumping her pillows, Jenny picked up one of the stack of Christmas novels she'd just bought and started to read, but she couldn't get into the plot and realized she was reading the same lines over and over. Snap. Trading one book for another, she tried to get engrossed in the story of a middle-aged woman who, on Christmas Eve, discovers that her husband is having an affair with a young colleague. Too close to home what with her stupid ex-fiancé's stunt from last year. No, thank you.

Sliding the second book back onto her To Be Read pile, she saw a stack of the catalogs Charlotte had left for Jenny in case she wanted to expand Garland's wardrobe.

The catalog entitled "Serene Home: Products for Getting Life under Control!" caught her eye. Heaven knew she could use serenity and control. Flipping it open, she found the section for goose clothes and couldn't believe the options.

Jenny grinned as she saw the brown pilgrim suit with the white collar, gold buckled belt, and black pilgrim cap. With Thanksgiving fast approaching, Garland *needed* this outfit. Hopping out of bed, Jenny grabbed her tablet and pulled a credit card from her wallet.

Once she'd warmed up by ordering the pilgrim suit, Jenny started clicking away. Into the cart went a seersucker suit with a plaid bowtie, just the attire for dressier occasions next summer. For Fourth of July, Jenny chose an Uncle Sam ensemble with a red and white striped top hat and white Abe Lincoln beard. The Statue of Liberty costume was darling but just too girly for Garland. Jenny selected the lifeguard outfit with the little whistle, and tennis whites accessorized with goose sunglasses and a miniature racket. Jenny broke into a smile when she saw a Santa Claus goose suit with the red jacket, black belt buckle, and sack of presents for the kiddies. That was a must buy.

Soon Jenny got intrigued with other clever items in the catalog, like a clock that lit up in the morning like a sunrise. Ageless beauty Sophia Loren endorsed a serum was guaranteed to banish the wrinkles on upper lips. Jenny ran a finger across the small road bumps on her own upper lip. Man, she needed that one.

Jenny also clicked the *Buy* button on several other items, the hummingbird feeder that stuck on a window with suction cups so she could see the little beauties close up, the chin strap for sagging jowls, and a pair of spikes she could buckle on the soles of her shoes and aerate the lawn by just walking around. Genius.

When she woke the next morning, Jenny saw the catalogs strewn across her bed and groaned. How many things had she bought last night? Scrubbing her face with her hands, Jenny groaned aloud. Who needed spike shoes to help aerate the lawn? Slipping on her robe, she gathered the catalogs for recycling and peered at the title.

Serene Home: Products for Getting your Life under Control. Jenny blew out a sigh. She knew what avid self-help reader and amateur life coach Charlotte would ask her. *Girly, what's going on in your life that's making you feel so out of control?*

Midweek, Jenny posted an ad on an online site called *Country Boy Buy and Sell* for a wagon that could serve as Santa's sleigh. One fellow from Selma had a wagon that sounded ideal until Jenny mapped the distance between Heron Lake and the little southern town. Three hours and forty-five minutes. How would she get there and get the wagon home? The logistics were not good. A women in Pinehurst claimed her rig used for harness racing would work just fine until she let slip that the cart only had seating for one. Another fellow claimed he had just the right wagon, but insisted Jenny wire him money before he delivered it to her. Sheesh. Jenny rubbed the bridge of her nose, and looked for other online buy-and-sell sites.

A knock sounded and Jenny was glad for the interruption. Glancing outside, she saw her young tenant, Lily, and smiled as she opened the door. With a red bow of a mouth, big green eyes, and her gleaming brunette ponytail threaded through a hole in her yellow fleece hat, Lily looked darling. A yoga mat strapped over her yellow jacket, the librarian and yoga enthusiast was probably on her way to the bluff where she did a late afternoon stretch most days.

"Hey there." Lily gave a shaky sigh, held out the key

to her cabin, and dropped it in Jenny's hand. "Tomorrow morning, two guy friends are bringing a truck to help me move. I hate to leave, but with Mama and Daddy letting me stay in their house for a year rent-free, I can really save up some money."

"I understand." Jenny felt a wave of sadness. She'd forgotten that Lily was moving out tomorrow. "I'm glad your folks' place is only two coves away so we'll be able to stay in touch. I want us to."

"Oh, absolutely," Lily said firmly. "You started as my landlady but now you're my friend."

Jenny swallowed a lump in her throat. "I feel the same about you."

Lily nodded so hard that her ponytail bounced. "I always keep up with my friends. Plus, I need to come visit on a regular basis just to see my fur babies." Stepping into the living room, Lily crouched and patted Bear, Buddy, and Levi, who responded by giving her adoring looks.

"Would you like to join me for a stretch?" Lily asked with a sweet smile.

Jenny eyed the gathering dusk and knew how cold it was getting now that the sun was going down. But this might be that last stretch with Lily in a long while. "I'll go with you." Jenny pulled on a jacket, hat, and gloves and grabbed her yoga mat.

Outside, the two women stepped off the composite walkway and walked briskly down the trail to the bluff. Jenny blew out a breath and watched it freeze. Winter was fast approaching. Puffing, she tried to keep up with Lily's pace. "So your folks are going to live in London for a year?"

"Yes. It's for Daddy's work. Mama's all excited. I'm taking a month in the spring to go see them and visit Ireland and Scotland, too." She gave a swooning sigh. "Maybe I'll be walking down a street in Edinburgh and run into a hunky actor like James McAvoy or Ewan McGregor who falls deeply in love with me." Her reverie faded, and she rolled her eyes. "But, as my ex-fiancé from Montana told me, long-distance relationships are for dreamers and fools."

"Your ex sounds like a prince," Jenny said drily. "Glad you didn't marry him."

They both were quiet for a moment as they picked their way down a path that had exposed roots that could be trip hazards.

"I want to save up to buy myself a little house. Daddy says that would be a good financial decision, and even though I want to get married, I'm just not sure it's in the cards for me," Lily said quietly.

"Always a good idea for a woman to have her own money and her own place." Jenny panted as they walked up a hill.

"Not everyone gets married," Lily said, sounding resigned.

Jenny glanced over at her young friend. Lily's broken heart had been healing this past year, but surely the right young man would come along and realize what a treasure she was. Lily might still be gun-shy around men though, and she lived out in the country where there might be slim pickings of available, suitable men. Then Jenny thought of Tom, kind, stable, wholesome- looking, unmarried Tom. Her brain began to whirl as her match-making instincts kicked in. Hmmm.

On the hike home after their gentle stretching and breathing routine, Jenny felt good. Rolling her shoulders, she breathed in the cold air and stepped lightly down the trail. "I got a lot of the knots worked out, and I almost feel five pounds lighter. Thanks, Lily."

"You're welcome." Lily stretched her arms over her head one more time. "I meant to tell you. We've gotten in heaps of new Christmas books at the library, the kind you like with strong heroines and happily ever afters."

Jenny pictured the stack of novels on her bedside table. Though she'd recently bought ten new paperbacks, one could never have too many good books at the ready. "Great. If you pick me out a few, I'll come by to pick them up."

"Happy to." Lily's walk had a bounce in it.

Jenny picked off a briar that tried to catch her jacket and shot Lily a questioning look. "We need a Christmas choir or chorus for the holiday, a musical group to per-form at the resort. Do you know of any?"

"Sure," Lily said blithely. "There's the children's choir from St. Elizabeth's who sound like angels. The women's choral group from the Heron Lake Ladies Club is very talented, and the choir from Bethel AME wins regional competitions every year."

Jenny stared at her. "Holy smokes. You're wonderful, Lily."

Lily dimpled, looking pleased.

"We'd like to invite the folks from the county to the musical performances and the visit from Santa," Jenny said.

Lily brightened. "I love that idea. I can help publicize it for you at the library. Maybe we can get Shandra Washington to do a feature about it in the *Heron Lake Herald.*"

"Any publicity would help." Jenny flushed, remembering that the last article about the Lakeside Resort had started with the catchy line, *Former Yuppie Gets Skunked.*

"Tell you what. Send me a list of songs you want to make sure the choral groups sing, and I'll see if I can set up a sort of audition for you. Let me make some calls," she said. "You can meet me at the library, and we'll go listen to each of them."

"Thank you, thank you, thank you," Jenny burbled and turned her gloved hands palms up. "We need music, but I didn't know where to start."

Lily gave a little skipping jump. "I'm a matchmaker for the choruses and the audience."

"You are." Enjoying her friend's exuberance, Jenny gave her a sideways glance. Lily was matchmaking, but Jenny was about to so some matchmaking of her own.

CHAPTER 7

L ATER THAT WEEK, JENNY WAS doing her usual morning routine of posting on social media, seeing if she had any nibbles or bites on the Welcome Inn reservation system, and checking correspondence. Quickly scanning her new emails, she saw one from Charlotte and smiled as she clicked it open. Her smile faded as she reread it.

Morning, girly girl. Sorry I've not been in touch, but I've been busy as all get out with this new job, but it's a ton of fun and I'm making moolah.

I've told Ashe I really do want to just get married at city hall. Much simpler and more practical.

No-over-the top wedding dress. Maybe that wench at the Elegant Bride was right, big dresses don't look good on big girls. I'll wear a simple off-white, knee-length ponte sheath. Most appropriate for my age, weight and sitch, too.

Am on a new diet, the Zoom Off the Pounds Diet. Involves a lot of positive affirmations, drinking a ton of water, and eating watercress soup.

How are Christmas plans going? How is that hunky Luke? I'll call or come see you soon.

Count on me to help with the Christmas soiree.

XOXOXO

Jenny sat back hard in her chair. Why had Charlotte changed her mind about everything? Suddenly, Jenny knew what had happened. Her scalp prickled with anger. That mean-as-a-snake Eugenie and all the other wenches who'd ever been mean to Charlotte about her weight had gotten in her head. With Eugenie's fat-shaming comments, she'd added to Charlotte's own doubts about her worthiness to celebrate her marriage just because she was over forty and had been married before.

Jenny shook her head in frustration. She knew Charlotte. Though her friend said she wanted a simple city hall wedding, she wasn't a no-fuss, no-muss bride who wanted to get married in street clothes at a charm-free municipal building. She'd seen her friend pouring over bridal magazines and studying them since her first date with Ashe. Her Pinterest board for wedding gowns was huge, and the dresses she loved were all extravagant confections. Yet, Charlotte was settling for a ponte sheath at city hall.

Let's talk about this. Call me when you get a chance," Jenny emailed back and sent the same message via text.

Though Charlotte usually responded immediately

to emails and texts, Jenny got no response. She called Charlotte twice but the calls went right to voice mail. Jenny pinched the bridge of her nose, thinking. She wasn't sure how she'd do it, but she was going to make sure Charlotte had the wedding she'd been dreaming about.

The issue with Charlotte stayed in the back of her mind throughout the day. The temperatures had dropped and now hovered around twenty degrees. Jenny kept the woodstove stoked and stayed toasty as she went about her work.

After she'd checked in the guests, Jenny pulled up her Welcome Inn reservation system again, her eyes widening as she saw more and more blue blocks that indicated cabins that had been booked. The trickle of holiday reservations had turned into a river. Jenny hugged herself, elated at the number of guests returning from last Christmas. Peg and her sister Lucy from Hollis, North Carolina, were coming back this year. The subject line read, *Hunting Widows No More!*

> *Hey, Jenny! We raved so much about what a great time we had last year with you all that our husbands are joining us this year instead of sitting in tree stands eating beef jerky and freezing their tails off! Any chance you could put us in side-by-side cabins? Any long weekend in December is fine. Looking forward to it!*

Daniel Wise, the widower with the two daughters, wrote:

The girls and I are looking forward to visiting you all again. Coming to the Lakeside Resort is our new Christmas tradition! And, by the way, thanks to you, Harriet and I are seeing quite a bit of each other and it's getting serious. Thank you, Jenny!

Hah! Next time Luke gave her a hard time about her matchmaking, she'd add Daniel and Harriet to her list of happily match-made couples. Jenny wrote a sticky note reminder to herself and stuck it on the corner of her computer screen. *Get Lily and Tom together!!!*

Slipping on a puffy jacket and wool hat, Jenny trudged outside to clean cabins. Music made cleaning go faster, and Jenny had her iPod tuned to the Golden Oldies Christmas Radio. By the time Johnny Mathis crooned *It's Beginning to Look a Lot like Christmas*, Jenny was starting to get in the spirit. She sighed as the King sang *Blue Christmas*, and sang along to the *blue, blue, blue* line. Bing Crosby came on, singing his silky version of *Walking in a Winter Wonderland*. Jenny paused and smiled, remembering that had been one of her parents' favorite Christmas songs. As she loaded the dirty linens into her shiny new, high-powered, high-efficiency washing machine, Jenny softly sang along.

Checking her phone several times, Jenny felt glum when she saw no response from Charlotte. Though she could be caught up with work, Jenny had a gut feeling her friend was avoiding her.

Jenny's Christmas decorations were stored in the laundry room, so she grabbed a big box and trudged back to her cabin. After four trips, Jenny brought the last box in and held her frozen hands out to steady heat emanating from the Nilsson. Room for heated storage space inside her own home might be nice. Another case for a larger cabin.

As she stopped shivering and her bones warmed, Jenny pulled ornaments from boxes and admired the floral arrangements she'd bought at an after-Christmas sale. The galvanized floral buckets that were tied with gold burlap ribbon held dried eucalyptus, red berries, blue lavender, and purple sage. They were lovely, and the scent of woods and flowers brought the outside in.

Jenny kept the music going. Andy Williams sang the cheerful classic *Happiest Time of the Year* as she checked her supply of wrapping paper. The sparkly white paper with the Scottie dogs dressed in plaid sweaters was so precious that she didn't want to wrap presents in it.

When Perry Como sang *Winter Wonderland* in that rich elegant voice of his, Jenny hummed along until she heard the line about the couple deciding to get married. She stood stock still and thought about it. She'd bet money that Ashe had no idea why Charlotte had changed her mind about the venue and dress, and he'd want to know the truth. It wasn't right that he *not* know and that the whole wedding day be one big compromise for Charlotte. Feeling a steely resolve, Jenny made up her mind. She wasn't going to let Charlotte settle.

If she was going to try to dissuade Charlotte from her boring, ultra-practical wedding, she didn't have much time. Charlotte was MIA and would likely try to stay that way. Even if Jenny tried to have a heart-to-heart with her, Charlotte was stubborn and would doubt Jenny if she told her she was worthy of more than a city hall wedding. The only person Charlotte would believe would be Ashe. Snatching up her phone, Jenny straightened her spine and dialed Ashe's law office. Her call went to voice mail.

"Hey, Ashe. It's Jenny. Will you please call me?" Jenny ended the call, her mouth suddenly dry as flour.

Ashe called back a half-hour later as Jenny watched a Lean Cuisine fish lunch spin around inside the microwave. "Hey, Jenny. It's Ashe here. Is Charlotte okay?" he asked, sounding breathless and slightly panicky.

"She's fine. I should have worded things differently. I'm sorry I scared you," Jenny said. Pausing, she took a breath and composed herself. "Can I come to Celeste and meet you for a cup of coffee? I think Charlotte might be pushing for a wedding at city hall for all the wrong reasons. I could be wrong, but I just wanted to run things by you."

"Gracious," Ashe murmured, clearly surprised by what she'd told him. "I'll clear my schedule and meet you anytime. Would tomorrow work?"

They made arrangements to meet at nine the next morning at a diner called the Corner Chat 'n' Chew. Jenny ended the call, admiring Ashe even more than she already did. That man loved Charlotte. The fact warmed her heart.

But her stomach clenched at the possibility that her little theory about Charlotte wanting a fancier wedding was wrong. She chewed a thumbnail and stared out the window at the choppy waves on the lake. There was a good chance Charlotte could get mad at her for interfering. But if she didn't talk to Ashe, Charlotte would end up not having the wedding she'd dreamed of.

Jenny lifted her chin. If it meant making Charlotte a happy bride, she'd take the risk and do it.

The next morning, Jenny threw a jacket over khakis and a cashmere crew neck and tooled up to Celeste. They'd had showers last night, so she drove extra carefully, wary of icy spots on bridges and shady stretches of roads.

With the help of Waze, Jenny found Corner Chat 'n' Chew, a homey-looking place with red-and-white gingham curtains and an old-timey neon arrow with the restaurant name on it.

Ashe was already seated in a corner booth. He stood when she approached and gave her a little hug. "Good morning, Jenny."

"Good morning, Mr. Mayor," Jenny said with a smile, noting he was dressing more nattily since he'd met

Charlotte. Instead of his wire glasses and tried-and-true navy-blue sports coat and tie, Ashe sported new hip-looking tortoise-shell glasses, a tweedy-checked sports coat, and a sophisticated brown and gold paisley bow tie.

"How are you and Luke and your mama and step-daddy doing?" he asked politely.

"We're fine. We're going fast trying to get ready for Christmas, but all is well."

A waitress dressed as a green-faced witch came by with a pot of fresh coffee and poured them each a cup. Startled, Jenny glanced around the diner and saw the scarecrow eating eggs and bacon and the vampire drinking a smoothie. She'd forgotten it was Halloween.

Jenny leaned forward. "Ashe, I'm worried Charlotte is trying to be too good a sport about the wedding and not having the day she really wants."

Ashe put down his coffee mug and studied her. "What makes you think that?"

Jenny summarized Charlotte's email about being practical. She tilted her head. "Charlotte told you about the mean woman at Elegant Bride?"

Ashe snorted. "She did. The owner was so unprofessional, I wrote her a stern letter."

"Good." Jenny meanly wished she could have seen Eugenie's face when she opened the letter from Ashe's law firm.

Pulling a copy of the glossy *Today's Bridal Style* magazine from her shoulder bag, Jenny showed it to Ashe.

"Charlotte left this in the Silver Bullet after her last visit." Flipping it open, she found the pages that Charlotte had favorited with a turned-down corner. The gowns she seemed to like best were glamorous, romantic, extravagant affairs with features like hooped skirts, long trains, billowing fabrics, and extravagant beading. One floaty diaphanous number looked to be Charlotte's favorite because in the column next to it, she'd used a red felt tip pen to scribble three stars and the words, *Perfect! Yes to this dress!*

Ashe stared at the photograph, looking confused. "So if she really wants a big dress, why did she tell me just the opposite?"

"You'll have to ask her," Jenny said.

"I sure misread her," he muttered. Looking shamefaced, he rubbed the back of his neck. "So, she wants a fancy dress. She doesn't want a large church wedding, a medium-to large-sized church wedding, or a simple city hall wedding. Do you know what she *does* want?"

"Nope, but you'll find out," Jenny said reassuringly, liking this man even more because he was taking her concerns seriously. "I just wanted to pass this on to you so you knew."

"I'm glad you did." Ashe sat up straighter. "I'll talk to Charlotte about this, but one thing I can tell you for certain. Charlotte deserves to have exactly the wedding she wants. There will be no city hall wedding in street clothes," he said firmly. "I can do better than that for my girl."

Back home, one of Jenny's favorite guests from last year, Viv from Southern Pines, had left a voice mail. Smiling, Jenny sank onto the sofa, leaned back, and crossed her legs as she listened, knowing she was in for a chatty but delightful message.

"Hey there, doll," Viv said in her big, throaty voice. *"Adored your newsletter. Loved seeing a picture of that little sugar bear, Levi! Sign us up for the winter sleigh ride! It sounds so merry and Christmassy! If it's frigid, I'll wear my big faux-fur hat and coat again and be toasty!*

"I'm bringing my knitting again. Be tickled to hold more informal all-gals' knitting clinics. Am I being naughty to suggest we enjoy an adult beverage while we knit?" she asked and chuckled.

"Hope we have another nice blizzard like last year. Slipping all over the road on the way to the resort was so much fun, just like when we lived up north. Kiss all the animals for me. Oh, and put us down from the 14th to the 1st. Let's make that a standing reservation every year. Let us know if we can help in any way. Retirement's making Hugh antsy, so if you have any projects for him, all the merrier for me!" She barked out that husky, unrestrained laugh Jenny loved. *"See you soon and kiss, kiss!"*

Jenny put her hands behind her head and smiled as

it dawned on her. These calls and personal notes from returning guests meant the Lakeside Resort was becoming an integral part of people's family holiday traditions, and many of her guests were becoming her friends. That thought warmed her.

Last year, by hard work, luck, and the wonder of four-wheel drive, they'd managed to pull off an extraordinary Christmas. She just needed another miracle this year. No pressure there, Jenny thought wryly, as she pulled up contact information for local stables and began making calls, asking for help finding a horse-drawn wagon.

For the next two days, Jenny didn't hear from Charlotte. She checked her phone obsessively, but no word. Radio silence. Jenny thought about losing Charlotte's friendship and her heart sank.

Throughout her work days, Jenny kept listening to Christmas music to try to keep from being down about Charlotte. Bing Crosby's *Silver Bells* was magical, and Perry Como's *Home for the Holidays* made her sing along. Frank Sinatra's *Ave Maria* and *The First Noel* gave her goose bumps and reminded her that faith was the reason for the season. When Nat King Cole sang *The Christmas Song*, Jenny scribbled *chestnuts* on her grocery list. She'd never tried chestnuts and would like to try roasting them on an open fire.

As the days passed, the fall leaves blazed even more

gloriously, temperatures dipped, and guests rolled into
the resort, eager for long, bracing walks followed by snug
and toasty fireside evenings.

Jenny was just responding to an inquiry about
December 7th when her incoming message alert dinged.
The text was from Alice, Luke's baby sister and one of her
favorite people. She wrote:

> Help. Lost in pregnancy land. Need a dose of u, the
> lake, the boys. When can I visit?"

With her wildly curling blonde hair and petite build,
some might see Alice as fragile, but the young woman
could swing a hammer, throw an axe, install a hot water
heater, lay hardwood floors, and with one look, keep
a classroom full of unruly kids on their best behavior.
Because Alice was a new graduate student and now a
new wife and mother-to-be, Jenny didn't get to see her
friend as much as she liked, and she'd missed her terri-
bly. Quickly, Jenny tapped out:

> Come tomorrow. I'll save the whole day for you. I
> need a dose of you 2!

Late Sunday morning, Jenny was sitting fireside, brush-
ing Bear and Buddy and trying to detangle their coats
when she heard the rumbling engine of Mike's big truck.
Smiling, she hurried out to greet her friends.

Lifting his trademark blue wraparound sunglasses

that looked like the ones the NASCAR drivers wore, Mike leaned out the window and gave her a friendly grin. "Hey, Jenny. How's it going?"

"Good, Mike." Jenny stood on tiptoes and bussed his cheek. "You ready for this baby?"

"So ready," Mike said, a note of desperation in his voice. He tilted his head toward Alice, who was unfastening her seatbelt. "My girl's had a rough go of things, Jen," he said quietly.

"Gotcha." Jenny nodded. "I'll take good care of her, Mike. We'll have a nice day."

A look of relief crossed his face. "That's just what she needs. I'll be back to pick her up at about two. Call me if anything comes up." He tipped up the brim of his ball cap and gave her a wicked grin. "I'm bringing you and Luke a little something I ran across."

"Good." Jenny was intrigued. To help supplement his income as a teacher, Mike did side jobs. In the winter, he plowed snow from parking lots. The rest of the year, he and a few teacher buddies operated a small moving company. Mike often brought home useful castoffs that clients didn't want or couldn't take to their new homes. Alice was proud of the finds he'd brought home, and what he couldn't use, he gifted to his friends. Last year, he'd brought Luke an almost brand new pig-cooker and a small lawn tractor. Both worked just fine.

While Mike solicitously helped Alice slide down from the high seat in the truck, Jenny worked to keep a neutral expression on her face. Pre-pregnancy, Alice'd had an effortlessly cool sense of style and looked darling in outfits Jenny would have never pulled off, pink overalls over a tank top, a ruffled dress with lace-up boots, or a red maxi dress with a bright orange jean jacket.

But today, besides the expected pregnancy weight, Alice's face was puffy and her eyes were swollen as if she'd been crying. Her hair hung dirty and lank around her face, and she had purple circles under her eyes. Worse, her friend was unsmiling and the twinkle was gone from her eyes. Alice looked depressed.

"So good to see you," Jenny said warmly, and leaned in to kiss her.

"I know I look awful, and I'm probably going to be terrible company," Alice said miserably. "I've been throwing up for months, yet I've still gained so much weight."

"I'm sorry, honey. Sounds tough." Jenny felt a wave of sympathy. Although she sometimes keenly missed having had children, Jenny wasn't sorry she'd missed this aspect of pregnancy. Putting an arm around Alice's shoulder, Jenny led her toward the cabin. "I fixed us chicken salad sandwiches, the kind you like with the grapes and the pistachios. I thought it if wasn't too cold after we ate, we could sit outside. We could bundle up, build a fire, and look at the lake. You always loved that. I'd take you on a boat ride, but your husband would strangle me and, our luck, you'd go into labor in the middle of the lake."

Jenny knew she was chattering but couldn't seem to stop herself.

Dull-eyed, Alice just nodded as they walked toward the house, not saying a thing.

CHAPTER 8

U NSURE OF HOW TO HELP Alice, Jenny started to bring her up to speed on news from the resort, but her friend just looked at her impassively until they reached the door of the cabin. Alice stopped short and grinned, pointing at Garland, who was wearing his pilgrim outfit. "I love your goose."

Finally. A way in. "Garland is his name. Charlotte gave him to me."

"Was he a thrift-shop find?" Alice asked, a spark of humor in her eyes.

"How did you know?" Jenny asked in a teasing tone. "I've ordered the little guy a Santa suit and other fun outfits."

"He's just precious." Alice awkwardly leaned down to pat Garland's head and broke into a smile. "He looks happy."

"I thought so, too. He's a glass-half-full kind of guy."

"Good." Alice managed a wisp of a smile. "Maybe the two of you can cheer me up."

Jenny breathed out a sigh of relief as they stepped inside the cabin. Good. Signs of life. Putting a pillow under Alice's legs, Jenny got her settled on the couch under a soft chenille throw blanket and fixed her a mug of herbal tea. Doing math in her head, she reminded herself that Alice was due at the end of December. Sinking into a chair, Jenny looked at her. "So, tell me. What's pregnancy been like?"

"Horrid." Alice had a haunted expression on her face. "I thought my pregnancy would be smooth. I was pretty fit and not that old. I thought I'd be one of those serene Madonna-like moms with the glowing skin, but I'm just not." She groaned and rubbed her belly. "After the first trimester, I thought things would settle down, but they got worse. I've felt nauseous all the time. My morning sickness lasted all day."

"I'm so sorry, sweets," Jenny said sympathetically, cringing inwardly just imagining it.

Levi walked over and put his head on Alice's knee. Cradling his head into her arms, Alice crooned, "Levi, my love. Where have you been these past eight months? I've needed you." Finally, she let him go. He stayed where he was, though, his head in her lap.

"Someone still thinks you're the most alluring woman in the world," Jenny pointed out.

"Levi, you are the best man." Alice actually laughed and wove her fingers through his mane. "I've thrown up in my sleep," she announced, her voice quavering. "I threw up during an award ceremony while the Dean was making the announcement for the statewide Educator of the Year. It was miserable and mortifying." She covered her face with her hands and started to cry.

Jenny scrambled for something genuinely comforting to say, but as a childless woman, couldn't offer one reassuring pregnancy story. As she handed her friend a box of tissues, their common ground came to her. Alice felt miserable and mortified. Recently having been dumped, evicted, and poor, Jenny *knew* misery and mortification, but she'd been saved by friends who understood her, didn't judge her, and stuck by her. "It's okay, Alice," Jenny said firmly. "Stuff like this happens."

Alice scowled, looking skeptical.

"Does the dean have children?" Jenny asked mildly.

Alice looked confused at the question and then nodded. "I think so."

"Are many of the other students in that assembly mothers?"

"A lot of them are." Alice gave a wisp of a smile and looked like she knew where Jenny was going with this.

"Do you think any of them had miserable pregnancies and got sick at inopportune times?" Jenny asked, praying she was on the right track.

Alice brightened. "A classmate told me she got sick

while she was defending her dissertation." She giggled. "Another upchucked when her husband was trying to get frisky."

They both started laughing.

Alice's shoulders dropped from where they'd crept up toward her ears. "I took a medical withdrawal from my graduate program," she said in a calmer voice. "Once I get so I can sit through a lecture without falling asleep or getting sick, I can continue my studies."

"There you go." Jenny gave her a reassuring smile. "I'm going to fix us lunch, and then we'll go outside and let those lake breezes just blow our cares away."

Alice gave her the first genuine smile of the day. "Sounds good."

By the time Jenny brought over the sandwiches, Bear was curled up at Alice's feet and Buddy had slithered between Alice's side and the cushions of the couch. Levi's head still rested on Alice's legs, and he sighed contently, secure in his knowledge that he was still the favorite.

As they munched the chicken salad sandwiches Jenny had made on flaky croissants, Alice's mood lightened. "My feet stay swollen as sausages," she said with a wry smile as she pointed past her stomach toward the general direction of her feet.

Jenny eyed her friend's feet. "Your ankles are a little sausagey, but not bad."

Alice burst out laughing. "I know. Mike calls them Jimmy Dean ankles."

Jenny cracked a smile.

Alice popped a bite of sandwich in her mouth and chewed it. "My shoes won't fit, so I've had to wear ter-rycloth house shoes like my nana used to wear." Again, she waved toward her feet.

"Comfort is *in* now." Jenny held up her foot, grateful she'd worn her clunky clogs that were heaven for her plantar fasciitis. "Look at my Little Dutch Boy shoes. Luke finds them *very* attractive." She wiggled her eyebrows up and down.

Alice snickered. "They *are* attractive." Handing Jenny her empty plate, she snuggled deeper into the couch cushions. "All right. I want to hear every detail about your life. Tell me about the resort, my brother, your wedding, Christmas, the whole thing."

Jenny paused. She'd always been open with Alice. "I love your brother more than I can even tell you, but I'm getting a few jitters about being married," she said tentatively. "I'm sure you didn't get nervous about marrying Mike..." She hesitated, gaping at her friend who had thrown her head back and begun whooping with laughter.

"You are so cute, Jenny." Alice choked out as tears of laughter trickled down her cheeks.

Jenny felt a wave of relief. "You're kidding. You had jitters, too?"

"Of course I did. That didn't stop me from wanting like mad to marry him," Alice said with a knowing look as she blotted her tears with a tissue. "Before Mike, I had a few rat boyfriends, men who ignored me or were critical or didn't get me at all." She rolled her eyes.

"Maybe that's what's going on with me. Ghosts of old, bad news flames," Jenny mused.

"Right." Alice gave her an understanding look. "And then there's the whole realization that hits you. *I'll be with this man the rest of my life.*" She gave an exaggerated shiver. "Mike can be bullheaded. We'll never have much money. Our politics are worlds apart." She shuddered. "He does not read. He doesn't get my jokes." Alice broke into a beatific smile. "All those thoughts raced through my head regularly right up until I said *I do* last Christmas."

"Regularly?" Jenny asked, disbelieving.

"Regularly." Alice bobbed her head. "But Mike loves me to pieces. He's smart and funny and endearing. He never looks at other women, puts up with my moods, and can fix anything. He's been so supportive during this pregnancy, and I have not been easy to live with." Her friend fixed her with a gaze. "Though I had doubts, I love him more and more each day."

Jenny found she was blinking back tears. "I'm so glad you told me this. It helps knowing other brides-to-be have felt that way, even though they know they've found great guys."

"Now you know the big secret. Lots of women feel that way," Alice said with smile.

After they'd finished eating, the two of them bundled

up and moved outside, sitting in the Adirondack chairs with windproof blankets and extra pillows for Alice. Though too windy to start a fire, the day was glorious, clear and bright with sunlight glittering like diamonds on the water. After they'd finished catching up with one another, the talk grew desultory.

Glancing over, Jenny saw Alice's head was bobbing, and soon her friend began to snore softly. Good. After her eight-month-long ordeal, Alice needed relaxation. Jenny adjusted the brim of her ball cap to block the sun and pulled the laptop from her bag. She'd answer email and follow leads for Christmas activities while Sleeping Beauty napped.

Later, Jenny heard the growling engine of Mike's truck and leaned over to gently shake Alice awake. "Hey, sleepy girl. Your husband's here."

Alice stretched, catlike. "What a restorative day."

"I'm glad." Jenny rose and reached down to help pull her from the chair.

Jenny followed Alice inside and helped her gather her coat and purse. After a heartfelt goodbye hugging session with Levi, Alice was ready to go. The two of them headed toward the truck. Mike had only pulled it partway into the driveway and Jenny wondered why.

Arms crossed, Mike leaned against the gleaming grill of his truck, looking pleased with himself. "Hello, my favorite ladies. How was the day?"

"Relaxing as a spa day, and your ears should be burning because I was saying such nice things about you." Alice reached up to give him a big kiss.

Mike shot Jenny a grateful look. "Sounds like just what the doctor ordered."

"It was," Alice said, still sounding a little sleepy from her nap. She gave Mike a questioning glance. "Did you get it?"

"I did," he said proudly. "Close your eyes, Jenny. We've got a surprise for you."

"Okay," Jenny said gamely and closed her eyes as the two of them led her up the driveway. After a few steps, they stopped. "You can open your eyes," Alice burbled.

And Jenny did, saw what Mike was towing behind the truck, and gaped at the small red-and-white vintage camper. Jenny lifted her sunglasses to get a better look, her heart fluttering with excitement. Though the compact travel trailer was encrusted in dirt, had two cracked windows, and was listing from a rear tire that had about gone flat, it was a beauty.

"It's a classic." Mike tilted his head toward the little camper. "I checked it out online. It's a 1956 Shasta canned-ham. It's just ten feet long and about seven-hundred-fifty pounds, but will be a little peach and roadworthy once you fix her up."

Resting a hand on the side of it, Alice's face was animated. "It's a little bit squat and not as sleek as the Silver Bullet, but it's cute as a button, and it's art and history rolled up in one. The Shastas were the most popular travel trailers from the 50s to the 80s. Today, they're still very popular and sought after by vintage RV fans."

"Wow," Jenny said reverently slowly circling the trailer and taking in the swooping curves and the triangular details. "Where in the world did you all find this?" With a finger, she rubbed the caked dirt off of the raised graphic that read, *Shasta*.

Mike beamed and hooked his thumbs in his pockets of his jeans. "We just helped a client clear out a falling down farmhouse that belonged to his daddy and mama. The Shasta was in an old outbuilding on the property. The guy said his daddy always intended to fix it up, but never got around to it." He gave a sideways grin. "This client's a nice guy, but he's a banker from Charlotte. Fancy clothes, fancy car. He has zero interest in this kind of thing. He told me to sell it for the metal and keep the cash."

Jenny cringed, imaging the camper going to the scrapyard. "I'm so glad you saved it."

"I sent Alice pictures of the camper, and she said you'd love it. It's in rough shape," Mike warned. "The mice have made themselves at home inside and eaten the upholstery. The roof leaks, and I can't vouch for the integrity of the floor. But Alice and I want you and Luke to have it if you want it. A gift from the two of us."

"Oh, my." Jenny put a hand to her chest, feeling overwhelmed. She wanted the camper so badly she could taste it, but could they in good conscience accept it? She'd seen the TV show about flipping campers. The Shasta had to be valuable. "Mike, this is too expensive a gift."

"Not in this poor a condition, Jenny. If you searched hard, you might find a camper that's in this bad shape and wouldn't pay much for it." Mike shrugged. "I got it for cleaning out an old double-wide packed to the rafters with junk. That job wasn't included in our original quote, so the Shasta was more like a tip."

Still not quite believing the camper might be theirs, Jenny took a step back, picturing it fixed up and used as a unique little guest cabin. Hipster or retro-loving guests would line up to stay in it. "I need to talk with Luke about it first, but we could do so much with this darling camper."

Mike carefully hooked an arm around Alice's neck and pulled her toward him. "You were instrumental in my getting off my backside and marrying this little gal. You threw us an excellent last-minute wedding last Christmas. Alice and I count you and Luke as two of our best friends, so let's just say this is an early wedding present."

"We love you, Jen." Alice smiled tremulously.

Swallowing a lump in her throat, Jenny flung her arms around the two of them. "Love you back."

After Mike promised to pick up the camper if Luke wasn't interested in it, he expertly backed it into a tree-lined corner of the property out of view of the cabins. He and Alice tooled off, waving from the open windows of the big truck before they closed them to keep the cold breeze out.

Walking back to the tiny camper, Jenny had a spring in her step as she examined it from different angles, imaging the dust and dirt scrubbed away and the red and white paint freshened and shining. Cleaned up and given some love, the camper would be just adorable.

Elated, Jenny tried calling Luke twice before remembering he was taking his dad to his last physical therapy appointment today. Fingers shaking, she sent him a quick text.

We got an amazing early wedding gift from Mike and Alice, IF YOU APPROVE. I love it but will tell you more later!!

Jenny couldn't stop grinning as she snapped several photos of the Shasta. Though she'd wanted to surprise Luke, she was just too excited to keep a secret. Attaching several of the best pictures, she sent him another text.

I think we may have found our Santa's workshop!

The next evening, Luke visited, his eyes bright with anticipation as Jenny led him to the Shasta tucked in the woods.

"Holy smokes. It's a pint-sized gem," he muttered, looking as intrigued with the Shasta as Jenny had hoped he'd be. Luke kept rubbing his chin as he walked around the camper. Pulling a small tape measure from his pocket, he measured the exterior to verify the dimensions, looked up Shasta specifications on his phone, and poked around inside, ignoring Jenny's pleas to be careful as he walked boldly around the saggy floor. "I'll start getting this baby cleaned up by the weekend," he said, looking like a kid on Christmas morning who'd just unwrapped the toy he'd been longing for. "After the dirt and grime is gone and the clutter inside is cleared out, I can size it up. New tires, of course. I can order those online. We can get parts from a vintage RV store. The first job is to reinforce these floors." He gave the camper a possessive pat. "This'll be a top-notch Santa's workshop."

Her hands on her hips, Jenny gave the Shasta another fond look. She was in love with the camper already. Narrowing her eyes, she tried to picture it as Santa's house. "I'll see if I can get Charlotte to find me a big, old thrift store chair for Santa to sit on."

"Good." In the fast-fading light, Luke continued to examine the Shasta, tapping out to-do list notes to himself on his cell.

Jenny pulled out her own phone. Her thoughts raced. Yesterday afternoon, she'd gotten a brief text from Charlotte that didn't tell her much. *Going 100 mph. Be in touch later. TTFN.* So curt for the usually ebullient Charlotte. She had to be furious at Jenny for talking to Ashe.

Breathing in a deep breath to try to calm herself, Jenny texted Charlotte.

Need ur help. Brand new to us vintage 1956 camper for

Santa's workshop. Need chair for Santa. Ideas? Jenny attached several pics and hit send, hoping the request would intrigue Charlotte enough that she'd overlook her spilling the beans to Ashe.

Soon, it was full dark. Luke put a hand on the back of Jenny's neck as they walked back inside to eat supper. He gave her a sideways smile. "You found your Santa yet?"

"No, but I'm working on it." Jenny held up crossed fingers, hoping the idea she'd had in the middle of the night might pan out. She'd make the call tomorrow.

Later in the week, Jenny was in the shower washing her hair when the phone rang. Hurriedly, she rinsed the conditioner from her hair and wrapped herself in a towel. She reached for the phone but the caller had hung up. Glancing at the display, she froze. Charlotte.

Slipping on a robe, she sat on the edge of the couch, her stomach now doing flips. She was a busybody, a meddler, a bad friend. But she had to face the music. Jenny summoned courage and hit redial.

"Hey, it's me. I'm on my way back to Celeste. Can I stop by?" Charlotte asked.

"Sure," Jenny said hurriedly. Her friend sounded harried, tense. Probably spitting mad.

"Be there in a minute. I'm right up the road," Charlotte said and ended the call.

Jenny threw on clothes and combed through her tangled hair, her breathing shallow. What if she'd ruined their friendship?

CHAPTER 9

A FEW MOMENTS LATER, JENNY HEARD the crunch of tires on gravel and hurried outside. Her eyes widened as she took in the approaching vehicle. Charlotte had decorated the sedan again this year, but she'd outdone herself. An almost full-sized Santa and his team of reindeer dashed across the top of her car in flashing red and green lights. If you suffered from migraines or epileptic seizures, it'd be best not to look at the car. "Hey, there," she called, trying not to sound nervous as her friend stepped out.

"Hey, yourself." Charlotte stuck her head back in the car, rummaged in the back seat and stepped out.

Jenny couldn't help it. Wringing her hands, she rushed over to the car. "Please don't tell me you're firing me as a friend for talking to Ashe." Jenny held her breath, waiting for her friend's response.

Charlotte's eyes widened, and she hugged her. "Girl, I am so not mad at you. I have just been going so fast that I don't even have time to eat lunch or go to the powder room." Releasing her, she looked at Jenny. "What would I do without you? Ashe and I talked, and we got it all worked out."

"Thank heavens." Jenny exhaled with a whoosh, aware she was grinning like a loon.

Charlotte smiled back but then gave her a stern look. "Promise me you'll rat me out again in the future if I need it, and I promise to do the same for you."

"Agreed. We each swear we'll rat each other out when necessary." Jenny held up three fingers, looking solemn, and Charlotte did the same.

Charlotte leveled a gaze at her. "There is nothing you can do to make me stop being your friend."

"Same here," Jenny said, her voice shaking with relief.

"Good." Charlotte said a nod of satisfaction. Briskly, she hooked a thumb to her car. "I found Santa's chair for eight bucks at the Episcopal Women's Thrift Shop. Help me get it out."

Thank heavens, Charlotte was back, Jenny thought as she reached in the car.

The two huffed as they struggled to extricate the large throne-like chair that Charlotte had managed to wedge into the car.

"It's just right." Jenny touched the soft red velvet arms and puffy velvet seat.

"Got that fabric and batting on sale and just stapled it in." Charlotte beamed proudly.

"This is the ideal Santa chair, both regal and comfy looking."

"I have an even better surprise," Charlotte announced, her face alight. She popped back into her car and emerged holding an envelope that she thrust in Jenny's hands. "Here. Special delivery." She hopped up and down with excitement as she watched Jenny open it.

Jenny pulled out an invitation. Printed in indigo blue calligraphy on a creamy matte paper, it was folded in laser-cut wrap that looked like lace. The whole thing was tied with a red velvet bow. Reading the simple words, she blinked back tears as she looked at Charlotte. "This is the prettiest wedding invitation I've ever seen and you picked the ideal venue."

Charlotte looked exultant. "I'm so glad, and I'm so excited. I have a thousand things to do in such a short amount of time." She gave Jenny a bone crusher of a hug and jumped back in her sleighmobile car. From the open window, she pointed at Jenny and called, "Sunday, December 1st. One o'clock sharp. I'll see you then."

Jenny blew extravagant kisses at her friend as she peeled away.

On the following Tuesday, Jenny's reminder ding went off on Outlook. She'd been thrilled when Lily wrote this weekend about having arranged the visit to the choral group and choirs. Jenny had invited Mama, and the two of them would meet Lily at the library and leave from there. As she pulled on her good black slacks and boots, she glanced out the window. Wearing her walking boot, Mama headed slowly toward the Dogwood on the new lakeside walkway.

The two women kissed, and Claire swung herself into the passenger seat of Jenny's eleven-year-old SUV with ease.

"Whoa, Mama." Jenny eyed her. "You seem so strong. Have you been working out?"

Claire proudly flexed her bicep. "I've been doing all the ankle, leg, and core strengthening exercises the physical therapist gave me. She said muscle tone goes in a snap at this age and since I've got to regain my ankle strength, I wanted to make sure I had arm and upper-body strength too. I've lost a little weight too," she said proudly.

"Good for you." Jenny glanced at her own pants that she'd only gotten into because she'd used a lying down, shimmying move that required two hands. As soon as things calmed down, she vowed she'd get into a regular, vigorous exercise program.

"Tell me all your news." Mama adjusted her car seat, sat back, and gave Jenny a look of bright interest that said she was ready for a good catch-up.

Jenny filled her in on Charlotte's news, their plans for the Shasta, and updates on the Christmas at the resort.

"This is all so exciting," Mama said with a happy sigh.

"I saw Landis head out. What's he up to today?" Jenny turned onto the state road.

Mama chuckled. "He's meeting his cronies at the convenience store. There's a barber in River Falls who's running a $7.00 special on haircuts. They'll all pile in the SUV and make the hour-long drive over there to take advantage of the bargain."

Jenny cracked a smile. As she understood it, all of Landis's cronies from Gus's were comfortable financially if not downright wealthy. "So, it's an excuse for an all-guy road trip."

"Correct." Claire smiled indulgently and went on. "On the way home, they want to stop at this greasy spoon that serves hot dogs with onions and slaw that will keep them up all night with heartburn." She shook her head. "This is their adventure for the day."

"Those retired men are pretty cute," Jenny mused.

"Landis is," Mama said, a smile playing at the corners of her mouth. "So Lily's taking us to listen to three groups singing?"

"Yup. If all of them are good, I'd like them all be a part of Christmas at the resort." She looked over at her mother. "Before I forget, let's try to throw Lily and Luke's new manager, Tom, together over the holiday. They could be a love match."

"Good." Claire reached over to pat Jenny's knee. She pointed out the window at the passing scenery. "How did I get this lucky? It's a crisp, cold morning. The trees are lit with color. We're going to the library, which I always love to do, and we're going to hear glorious Christmas music. Best of all, I get to spend this whole day with my daughter."

Jenny smiled at her and mulled it over, trying to decide if she should bounce her wedding jitters off Mama as well. Full steam ahead. "Let me ask you something, Mama. Luke is an amazing man, and I'm so grateful and happy that he wants to marry me. But for some reason, I'm having trouble getting excited about the wedding and about building the new house."

Claire gave a matter-of-fact nod. "Well, you've had so much going on, and it's going to get even more hectic before your big holiday event. Do you think that's it?"

"I'm not sure." She glanced over at her mother. "Do you think it's wedding jitters? I know you just knew Landis was the one early on and didn't look back..."

Her mother burst out laughing. "Oh, darling. I was married to your father for nineteen years, a man who loved me to pieces but always, and I mean always, let me down." She threw up her hands. "I was *so* skittish about love."

Jenny was genuinely surprised but remembered a period after her parents' divorce during which she wouldn't speak to her mother, blaming her for divorcing Jax. It was only later that she understood that only a saint or a martyr would have stayed married to Jax, that charming but reliably unreliable rambler. "But I thought you met

Landis in the waiting room of your dentist, and it was love at first sight. Things just took off."

Claire shook her head so hard her dangly chandelier earrings tinkled. "Oh, no. Things didn't take off. They sputtered, stopped, got thrown into reverse, and stalled. Landis had to be so steady and patient until I finally started to believe that our love might be real and might last. I'm surprised he didn't just throw up his hands and find an easier woman to love."

Hunh. This was big, important news. Jenny was quiet for a moment, considering it. "Why don't women tell each other this stuff? Everybody acts like being engaged is all a sea of love, but it's a huge change."

"And a leap of faith." Her mother slipped on sunglasses. "After being disappointed by love, it's hard to trust again. And you had that experience with that awful shallow Douglas. It makes sense to me that you'd be apprehensive, but that doesn't mean Luke's not your guy. I adore that man and think he's such a good fit for you."

"I do, too. Thanks for telling me about your experience, Mama." Jenny put the blinker on and changed lanes, her mind racing. "I need to think about that."

"I'm glad it helped. Maybe talk about it with Luke. Even the smartest men sometimes need a little help understanding things like this."

"I will." Jenny was grateful for the open way Mama talked with her.

Lowering the window, Claire took several deep

breaths of the chilly morning air and intently studied the vibrantly colored tree line. Leaning her head back in the seat, she closed her eyes. "I just want to bottle all this fall brilliance so I can hold onto it forever. I'm going to try to memorize every little nuance of this color so I can try to recreate it on canvas."

At the library, Lily rushed over and greeted them warmly. "I just need a few more minutes, and I'll be ready to go," she said apologetically as they dodged the children and parents swarming into the room for story time.

Jenny picked up the stack of novels she'd requested. With those and the ones she'd bought, she should have a good reading supply for the holidays.

Mama headed to the Arts Section, walking around in her boot like a pro.

Jenny ambled over to the Travel Section and browsed, her finger trailing across the spines of books, reading titles. Her talks with Luke about their honeymoon had just been preliminary. She needed to get ideas. Jenny browsed the book titles. *Train Trips across the U.S., The Best Coastal Road Trips, Civil War History Tours,* and *Lighthouses of America.*

Savvy librarian Lily also had sections called Bring Fido Along: Travel Guides for Pet Owners, Disability Friendly Getaways, and a section called Happy Honeymoon Destinations. Jenny's heart ticked up a beat, and she wondered at the coincidence of it. Maybe God and Jax were giving her a little inspiration today. Heaven knows, she needed it.

Greece looked to be a popular destination, but that's where she and Douglas had planned to honeymoon. Positano on the Amalfi Coast of Italy looked like a post-card, but she vaguely recalled that Luke and his late wife had vacationed there. The Caribbean, Bermuda, and Costa Rica all looked inviting but, between her and Luke, they'd each been to many of those places, either as single adults or with other spouses. That was the trouble when you married later.

Jenny picked up a book called *Rockin' Honeymoons* and eyed the glamorous, physically flawless couples in their mid-twenties nuzzling each other on balconies, lying practically on top of each other on lounge chairs while holding coconut drinks, and floating in endless pools while gazing hungrily into each other's eyes. Sheesh. Be nice to have cover photos of middle-aged honeymoon-ers, a crowd that she knew was a sizable demographic because she'd skimmed an article about it on her MSN homepage. She'd prefer to see men with dad bodies and women with fluffy waistlines and thighs.

Jenny was about to give up and go find Mama when she spotted several books on camping, including a travel guide called, *The Most Scenic and Romantic RV Camping Destinations in the South.* Feeling a flutter of excitement in her chest, Jenny flipped through it, her heart catching at stunning color pictures of a normal, non-glamorous-looking couple smiling at their campsite beside a rushing creek. A plump-ish pair embraced under a waterfall. A fellow in his sixties who wore a bucket-shaped canvas hat had his arm around his gray-haired wife's shoulder as they took in a stunning long-range mountain view in the North Georgia Mountains. A contented-looking couple tooled down the Natchez Trace in their truck, pulling an old camper that had seen better days.

Jenny held the book to her chest, feeling elated as she imagined an adventure in the Silver Bullet. She and Luke could find scenic, inspiring places and stay a while. Maybe they'd visit some of her buddies from the *Small Hoteliers and Innkeepers Forum* that she belonged to, the hoteliers who'd given her such helpful advice and support this spring as she tried to figure out how to draw guests to the resort.

Jenny's excitement grew as she thought of visiting their unique properties, the motel that consisted of twenty teepees, the ten rental treehouses, the B&B in the converted lighthouse. Maybe they'd even head out west. She could meet friendly Bertha and see her motor court of vintage RVs. They could visit Zig and tour his old-timey motor court of chalet-style rooms near Yellowstone.

A flutter of excitement in her chest, Jenny took several travel guides from the shelves and clutched them to her chest as she went to check them out. Finally, she could start to picture her honeymoon. If Luke was on board, they'd take the Silver Bullet on the trip of a lifetime.

The children's choir from St. Elizabeth's *did* sound like angels. Dressed in red robes with white collars, they fidgeted while the organist talked with Jenny about song selection. From the corner of her eye, Jenny saw a little red-headed girl poke her neighbor with an elbow. A boy with a mop of unruly hair sneezed and wiped his nose on his arm. Two fellows who looked to be identical twins had a brief shoving match. The choir did not look like angels, but when they opened their mouths to sing, oh, my. Dulcet-toned, soaring sweetness. The hair on the back of Jenny's neck stood up, and she broke out in goose bumps.

Their voices were pure and true, and based on the song, alternately hushed, reverent, and joyful. *Do You Hear What I Hear* and *What Child Is This* touched Jenny so that she shivered. When they sang *O Holy Night*, Jenny was not the only one wiping tears from her eyes. When the soaring stopped and the last note faded, Jenny clapped so hard her hands hurt. She looked over at Lily and shook her head in admiration. She turned to the pianist and choir director. "We'd be so honored if your children came to perform for us."

The women's choral group from the Heron Lake Ladies Club were a lively and talented group. Their music was a mix of religious and secular, and Jenny found herself wanting to sing along to a few numbers. The choir director, a stocky woman with a megawatt smile, offered a little commentary and factual tidbits before many of their songs. *"Brenda Lee recorded this hit when she was only thirteen years old,"* she said as the bright-faced gals swung into a high energy, fun version of *Rockin' Around the Christmas Tree.* "That song and the next were written by a Johnny Marks. An American songwriter who was Jewish, Mr. Marks wrote many hit Christmas songs," she explained as the chorus broke into a rousing version of *A Holly Jolly Christmas.*

When they'd finished, Jenny beamed and reached out to shake the choral director's hand. "Please come sing for us."

The choir from Bethel AME gave the other choirs a run for their money, but their sound was more soulful and emotional. Voices lifted and arms were raised as they sang *Away in a Manger, What Child Is This* and *Mary Did You Know.* Afterward, when Jenny approached the choir director, she laid a hand over her heart. "We would love to have you all be part of our Christmas celebration."

The next evening, after she fed the boys, Jenny poured herself a glass of wine and sat down at the computer. Taking a fortifying sip, she pulled up the cabin designs that Luke had tried to interest her in, and really looked at them. Leaning closer to the screen, Jenny found herself getting drawn in. She pulled out a piece of paper so she could scribble down her thoughts.

One of Luke's top priorities was that the cabin be designed so they could easily add an annex to it that could be used as the Guest Check-In and Office. Jenny wanted the two of them to have as much privacy as possible; ideally, to be completely out of the line of sight from the guests. She'd like to not worry about changing out of her nightgown and robe in the mornings as she drank coffee on the porch and looked out at Heron Lake.

Jenny and Luke had both agreed that the kitchen and the master bedroom had to have full lake views. Jenny wanted space between the master and the two guest rooms, maybe even a split floor plan. She recalled staying in a friends' guest room situated on the same end of the house as her hosts' bedroom. With the rooms so close, she was kept awake by her friend's husband snoring.

At the pizza meeting, Luke had pointed out that the twelve-foot ceilings made the rooms seem more spacious, and Jenny agreed. All logs throughout the interior was too dark. They needed to put sheetrock up on a few walls and paint them a sunny color. Maybe they could get skylights put in. Would solar tubes work in a cabin to make a dark room light?

Jenny's neat handwriting became a hasty scrawl as she got clearer and clearer on her preferences. Now all she had to do was look at the 3-D images of the four cabins again, and she'd know the one.

The days flew by the way they tended to as the year wound down. Before Jenny knew it, it was Thanksgiving.

The turkey dinner she'd ordered from Slowpoke's Diner was delicious. The turkey was moist and flavorful. The sides, whipped sweet potatoes with caramelized marshmallows, sautéed Brussels sprouts with pancetta, charred green beans with lemon, and herbed oyster stuffing, were scrumptious and zestier than the usual Thanksgiving fare. The bourbon pecan, apple, and pumpkin pies were as tasty as any Jenny had ever baked herself. Slowpoke's had delivered a meal that far exceeded the level of cooking that Jenny had expected to find out in the country more than two hours from Charlotte, the closest metropolitan area.

Mama, Landis, Luke, and his parents, Frank and Caroline, joined her for supper at the Dogwood. Frank was looking well, Jenny thought, as she passed him the potatoes. He was walking more straight and steadily. The side of his mouth that had gotten drawn up by the stroke seemed to have relaxed a bit. Frank's speech was slow, though, and he got caught on certain consonants, but the twinkle was back in his eye, and he and Caroline seemed closer than ever. When Jenny dropped a fork and bent down to retrieve it, she was touched when she saw that the two held hands under the table.

"How are the special events for Christmas coming along?" Caroline asked.

She shot Claire a smile and raised both hands in victory. "Thanks to our friend, Lily, we've lined up amazingly wonderful choirs and a choral group for Sunday evenings during weekends in December." Jenny looked at Landis. "If you'd help me get songs set up on your iPod, we can do our own caroling."

"Be happy to," Landis said. "How about Santa and the wagon rides?"

"I've got a tentative yes from Santa," Jenny said, trying to look mysterious, but then heaved a sigh. "Still no luck so far on the wagon."

"Sorry I couldn't help, shug," Landis said, frowning. "As it turns out, my buddy's son sold his horses, but he offered to lend us two elderly mules. I've always liked mules," he said fondly, his mouth crooking up. "But I don't guess that's the look you were going for."

Bemused, Jenny shook her head no.

Luke chuckled. "Tom and I went out to look at a wagon one of our customers offered us. He hadn't mentioned that it had been in the barn for thirty years. It has a broken axle, squirrels had eaten the seat away, and it only had one front wheel." He shrugged, his eyes full of mischief. "Other than that, it was in mint condition."

Jenny laughed with the others, but then pointed a finger first at Luke and then at Landis. "You two men need to stay on the hunt," she said lightly, but she was worried. "We have guests counting on wagon rides, and I'd hate to disappoint them."

Frank held up his hand, and they all turned to him. He gave an uneven smile. "I know a f-f-f-fella who might c-c-could help."

CHAPTER 10

S UNDAY MORNING, JENNY DID A few back and shoulder stretches as the coffee brewed. Opening the blinds, she gasped with pleasure. The ground was covered with a light dusting of snow. With a backdrop of the white-covered foothills in the distance and a mist hanging several feet above the slate blue of the water, Heron Lake looked magical. All guests had fires in their woodstoves, and the smoke drifting lazily from the stone chimneys made the cabins look even more cozy, toasty, and inviting. But Jenny had a worry. Today was Charlotte's wedding day. Would the roads be bad? Would guests be able to get to the venue?

Clutching her flannel robe close, Jenny poked her head out the door of the cabin. Hmm. Warmer than she thought. Glancing at the old red Texaco pump thermometer hung on the cabin, she saw it was 34 degrees. A soon as the sun came full up, the snow would melt. The wedding should go off without a hitch.

Buzzing with childlike excitement at the first snow of the season, Jenny felt a wave of nostalgia as she remembered sledding down a steep snowy hill with her dad. If school got canceled for inclement weather, Mama would bake white chocolate chip cookies. Jenny remembered the delicious scent of them baking and the pleasure of the taste and feel of still-warm cookies melting in her mouth.

After Bear and Buddy had finished wolfing down their kibbles and Levi had chewed the last of his breakfast, Jenny peered at the snow again. She'd take a walk with them and snap pictures of the swirling, sparkling white stuff. If she put the photos in a brief newsletter and sent it to guests who'd made reservations, she'd get them jazzed about their visit to the Lakeside Resort. Jenny threw on warm clothes, grabbed her camera, and she and the animals headed outside.

All three of the boys were pepped up with the temperature change, and the dogs were enthralled with the snow. Bear dropped to roll in it, and Buddy followed suit. Levi had his doubts about the white stuff, stepping daintily through the half-inch that had accumulated and glancing repeatedly at Jenny for encouragement. After taking several fun shots, Jenny headed home, feeling pure happiness as she thought about Charlotte and Ashe preparing for this afternoon. Today was going to be a blue-ribbon day.

After she'd showered and blown dry her hair using an expensive serum that promised to make her hair *gleam like burnished gold*, Jenny carefully applied makeup. These days, her morning beauty routine consisted of slathering on moisturizer and beauty balm with a 50 SPF rating, so Jenny was out of practice getting dolled up. Poking her eye with a mascara wand, she waited for the tearing to stop before she tried again, brushed on blush, and slicked on a ruby red lipstick. There. She checked herself in the mirror. She looked pretty good for her mileage.

Her heart ticked up a beat when she heard Luke's truck. Smoothing the front of her green velvet fit-and-flare dress, Jenny teetered a little on her heels and tried to remember how to walk in shoes other than comfortable boots and sneakers. Hurriedly, she hooked on small dangly pearl earrings and fastened the clasp of a pearl necklace that had belonged to her grandmother. Slipping on her winter dress coat, she blew a kiss to the boys and hurried to open the door.

Yowsa. Jenny's eyes widened as she took in Luke in his finery. Usually he was in jeans and work boots, and Jenny adored his casual, outdoorsy man's man look, but when the man dressed up, he looked like a million bucks. Freshly shaven, he'd neatly combed back his slightly too-long hair so it brushed his collar. With his tall, rangy build and broad shoulders, he simply wore clothes well. In a camel hair overcoat, the blue-green Burberry check plaid scarf draped around his neck made his eyes looked almost teal this morning. "You look like a movie star. A Brad Pitt, younger Harrison Ford combo," she said in a matter-of-fact tone and leaned in for a kiss.

"And you are breathtaking." Cupping her face in his hands, he kissed her slowly, tenderly, thoroughly. His eyes never leaving hers, he tucked a loose strand of curl behind her ear. "It'll be our turn for a walk down the aisle before we know it," he murmured.

Jenny closed her eyes and leaned into Luke for a moment, feeling both safe and euphoric at the thought of being with him forever. "I can't wait," she said softly." She slipped her hand in his, and they headed out.

Luke opened the door of the truck for her and gave her a hand as she clambered up to the seat. Snap. It was hard in those heels.

Luke started the engine. "So, I've got that we're headed to Asheville, but where is the wedding going to be held?"

Jenny fiddled with her phone to get the address in Waze. "The wedding, reception, and supper are being held in an old tobacco warehouse that was converted to retail. It's called *Flights of Fancy Thrifty Antiques*." Jenny gave a satisfied nod. "It's one of Charlotte's favorite stores, and it suits the two of them so much better than city hall."

Luke broke into a smile. "I know the place. It used to be called the Burley Warehouse, and that's where they held the tobacco auctions every year."

Jenny tilted her head. "So how exactly did the auctions work?" Not having grown up in a family that farmed, she had holes in her knowledge of this history.

"Every fall, the growers and the buyers would meet for the auction. The tobacco got brought in on tractors towing flatbed trailers. The auctioneer would chant as he walked down the rows where the bales were stacked, and buyers would walk behind him, sizing up the tobacco and nodding or winking to make their bids." Luke's voice was animated as it always was when he talked about history. "The prices got settled right on the spot. It was a real colorful event that happened every year," he said, sounding nostalgic. "North Carolina still grows two-thirds of the tobacco in the country, but these days, most of it's sold under contract. The growers deal directly with the tobacco companies."

"Why did the auctions stop?"

"They started to die out when the government stopped price supports for tobacco. Some folks left farming, but other farmers just left tobacco and moved on to other crops, like cotton, soy beans, sweet potatoes, and corn for grain." Luke slowed the truck to let a car merge in the lane in front of him. "The hemp and CBD market is taking off, and you've got a small percentage of growers moving to organic crops to sell to farm-to-table restaurants. I've even seen fields of lavender growing Down East. So, farming's a lot more diverse now."

Jenny enjoyed his tutorial. Luke wasn't a chatty guy,

but when he did talk, he was so knowledgeable. "How do you know all this stuff?"

"Remember, Daddy and my granddaddy use to farm tobacco. I used to help out, and they'd take me to the auction." He gave her a one-sided smile. "That was hot, dirty work. Made me know I wasn't tough enough to want to grow up and farm."

When they arrived at Flights of Fancy Thrifty Antiques, Jenny and Luke headed inside.

"These are sweet," Luke said admiringly as he pulled open the twenty-foot-tall doors to the building. "The doors had to be tall because the tractors pulling bales of tobacco on trailers would drive right in here."

"Huh," Jenny said, picturing it. "The floors are cool, too." She looked down at the beat-up but still gleaming wide-oak planks that dipped a little in spots.

Holding hands, they wove their way through the front of the store toward the back where they heard voices. Glancing up, Jenny smiled when she saw a large replica of the propeller-driven biplane Orville and Wilbur had flown near Kitty Hawk. Beside her were stacks of antique wooden steamer trunks with colorful luggage labels attached, a row of old guitars, and a glass case full of antique perfume bottles. Next to that was an eye catching display of vintage women's hats. Jenny slowed to admire them, boaters festooned with red, white, and blue nautical ribbons, blue-green plumes of feathers on fedoras, cloches adorned with fabric roses, and coquettish fascinators with bejeweled veils.

Luke led her into the back room. About fifty guests milled about, greeting each other and sipping flutes of bubbly. The room was large and high-ceilinged. There were no rows of chairs arranged like they'd be at an outdoor wedding, but banquet tables were set up off to the side. Jenny guessed they'd stand for the ceremony and then sit down at the tables to eat together afterward.

White-aproned waiters were finishing arranging place settings on a line of four long trestle-style tables covered with creamy damask tablecloths. Peonies, roses, and hydrangeas brimmed from tin buckets placed strategically down the table, and two pink crystal chandeliers hung over the tables. In a corner of the room, a group of black-jacketed musicians with violins, basses, flutes, and horns tuned up and began to play.

She was expecting Bach's Prelude in C or a similar song she'd heard at almost every wedding she attended, but the musicians launched into a soulful instrumental version of the Beatles' *I Saw Her Standing There*. Jenny broke into a smile as she caught the eyes of other guests who seemed surprised and delighted by the choice. Jenny knew Ashe was a music buff with a thing for oldies and a range of music he enjoyed. The tunes today ought to be interesting.

Jenny grinned up at Luke. "Nothing traditional about

our girl. She and Ashe are doing what they want, and I love it."

Luke put an arm around her shoulders. "Glad you meddled."

Jenny gently poked him with an elbow.

The two went over to say hello to Charlotte's parents, who greeted them warmly. Nell dabbed brimming eyes with a crumpled tissue. "I can't believe I'm crying already, but I'm just so happy. Charlotte's walking on air, and Ashe is the man I've always dreamed of for my girl."

Her husband Beau patted her back. "I'm just happy Ashe is employed and not as an artist," he said dryly, and Nell started to chuckle through her tears. "It's a happy, happy day, my love," Beau said and dropped a kiss on top of his wife's head.

Touched by their exchange, Jenny and Luke drifted off as the musicians segued into Marvin Gaye's *How Sweet It Is to Be Loved by You*. They went to greet Mama and Landis, who'd driven separately so they could go home whenever Mama got tired of standing. Mama looked beautiful in a cobalt blue lace midi dress. Holding Landis's arm, she looked relaxed and confident with one sturdy oxford on her good foot and the boot on the other. She kissed both Jenny and Luke, and clasped her hands together. "I just love weddings."

Elvis Presley was singing *Can't Help Falling in Love with You*, and Jenny swayed to the music. Glancing around, Jenny recognized several of Charlotte's besties from her Interior Design and Staging classes at the community college. One luminous young woman had a platinum crewcut and wore a gold lame evening dress. The other, a Taylor Swift lookalike, had a tall beehive and wore a floral 1950's-era dress with a full skirt. Jenny smiled, admiring their youthful offbeat beauty as they rocked what were probably thrift store finds. She waved and walked Luke over to say hello, reminding the two of who she was. "Luke, these are the talented young women who helped Charlotte completely freshen up Daddy's house in Celeste and get it ready to go on the market. They really are responsible for it selling."

The young women's carefully blank expressions and auras of cool boredom melted at the compliments. The white blonde beamed. "Bible, it was Gucci."

"TD," the other said. "I loved the aesthetic."

Luke looked baffled. Jenny had no idea what they meant, but knew they were nice young women. She decided to just beam at them. "You both are just darling, and you've raised the hipness factor of the wedding party way up. We thank you for that." With smiles all round, Jenny and Luke drifted off.

The Dixie Cups' *Chapel of Love* came next, and Jenny saw a few of the older couples looking nostalgic and singing along.

The two of them introduced themselves to others, Charlotte's aunts, uncles, and cousins and a small group of relatives from Ashe's side of the family. A woman wearing a name tag and holding a clipboard approached Jenny with a smile. "I'm Hannah from Hannah's Catering. The bride asked to see you." She pointed. "She's behind that screen in the little alcove."

Jenny gave Luke's hand a squeeze and hurried back to the alcove. When she saw Charlotte, she gasped and put a hand to her mouth. Charlotte was wearing the dress from the page she'd turned down in *Today's Bridal Style* magazine, the frothy confection with a big train, crystals, and pearls sewn into the bodice. "You are the most gorgeous bride ever," Jenny breathed and twirled a finger. "Turn around so I can get the full effect."

Pink-cheeked with pleasure, Charlotte held out both hands and slowly twirled around.

"You look like an angel on the top of a Christmas tree. You're an *elegant* bride with a groom who adores you." Jenny's voice shook with emotion.

Charlotte teared up and dabbed at her eyes with a lace handkerchief. "I don't want to cry and ruin everything." Smiling, she fanned her face with her hands. "I just wanted to say again how grateful I am for your stepping in."

"Butting in," Jenny corrected, with a wry smile.

"Stepping in." Charlotte touched her arm. "For our honeymoon, we're going to St. Lucia to stay in one of those bungalows over the water. And later this year, Ashe has promised we can go stay at one of those ice igloo hotels. I've always wanted to do that."

"Good for you," Jenny said. It was a joy to just look

at Charlotte. Her friend was animated, glowing, and just plain radiant. A picture perfect bride.

"We'll just be gone two weeks." Her friend held up three fingers in a Girl Scout promise sign. "I promise we'll be back in plenty of time to help you with Christmas."

Jenny felt a wave of relief. "I'm glad, girl. I want you to have a fabulous honeymoon, but I don't think I can pull off this holiday without you." Careful not to smudge her friend's makeup, Jenny leaned in and kissed her cheek. "I am so happy for both of you."

"Thanks, sweets." A beaming Charlotte gave her a finger wave, and Jenny couldn't stop smiling as she headed back to the others. It was thrilling to see Charlotte so utterly happy.

Ella Parr's retired Episcopal minister husband Paul walked into the room in his crimson and gold vestments. With a beatific smile, he waited until the musicians had finished the processional, Roy Orbison's *Pretty Woman*. As the last note faded away, Ashe walked into the room with a beaming Charlotte on his arm. He wore a cutaway tux and a bowtie, and Charlotte's dress rustled and swished as she walked. A collective gasp rose from the crowd as they saw the couple and someone began to clap. The others joined in until it was almost deafening. Charlotte put her hands up to her cheeks, laughed, and leaned her shoulder into Ashe's. When the clapping quieted, Paul stepped forward and began in his rich baritone. "We are gathered together..."

The couple's vows were simple and sincere, and when Paul pronounced them husband and wife, cheers erupted from the crowd. After more mingling and congratulations, the guests took seats at the long trestle tables. Waiters served glasses of wine and Prosecco as the caterers spun into action. After a crisp salad of mixed greens topped with tiny cherry tomatoes, bacon, candied pecans, and crumbled goat cheese, the main course was fresh scallops on a bed of braised Swiss chard with sides of tender asparagus sautéed in butter and drizzled with lemon and tiny, tender fingerling potatoes. After they'd eaten, Charlotte and Ashe cut the cake, half carrot, which was Charlotte's favorite, and half coconut, Ashe's favorite. "A his and hers cake," Ashe announced as he tenderly fed Charlotte a morsel.

As they drove back to Heron Lake, Jenny looked out the window, feeling a lightness in her chest. The radio was on and Ella Fitzgerald sang the classic Christmas song, *I've Got My Love to Keep Me Warm*. Jenny listened intently, hearing the lyrics like it was the first time she'd heard the song. She *got* the song's sentiment about a strong love making you feel safe, warm, and sure about the future. Strong love made you feel like you'd come home. Luke's face was lit by the dashboard lights, and she studied him, noting his familiar handsome profile, the strength of his fingers lightly gripping the wheel, the careful way he drove down the winding mountain road to make sure they got home safely. Safety, sureness, fire, home. That's what she had in Luke.

"Can we talk about our future?" she asked.

Luke hesitated. "Okay."

"You seem surprised," Jenny said with a half-smile.

"Whenever I bring up our future, you get all rabbity and scared. You change the subject."

"I know. I'm sorry," Jenny said quietly. She fiddled with the strap of her purse. "I've also been rabbity about picking out the cabin and the thought of moving."

Luke just nodded.

"I've realized that I'm still a little spooked by love. Not because of you," Jenny said hurriedly. "You are the *best* man, and I am sure of my love for you and yours for me." She stared out the window unseeingly. "I think it's just the old fears about being abandoned. First Jax abandoned me on a regular basis. Then my first husband left and Douglas disappeared." Jenny's mouth was dry from nerves but she made herself go on. "But I've managed to find such a kind, trustworthy, true-hearted man." She held her hands palms up. "What I'm going to do is trust all this data you have given me, your feelings, your constancy, and your big, generous love. I'm not going to let fears make me scared anymore." Jenny glanced over at him. "If I get scared, I'll talk to you about it."

"Good. About time." Luke looked at her intently. "Jenny Beckett, I will always love you with all my heart and never, ever leave you. No matter how rabbity you get, you couldn't run me off if you tried."

Jenny felt her eyes prickle with tears. "Love you, baby boy."

"I love you, Jen," Luke said gravely.

"So I have three things to say to you," Jenny said crisply, and held up three fingers. "One. Let's honeymoon in the Silver Bullet. Let's start our lives together with a grand adventure."

"Great idea." Luke beamed. "That was my top pick, but I wanted you to be the one to decide."

"Two. The Blue Ridge. That's the cabin I like best."

Luke threw his head back and laughed. "That cabin had the best arrangement of space, more storage, and was just plain prettiest."

Jenny grinned, pleased at his reaction. She held her fingers back up. "Three. June 20th. Let's get married June 20th."

Luke let out a whoop and hit the steering wheel with the palm of his head. "June 20th it is, darlin' girl."

A light snow began to fall, swirling, sparkling, and dancing in the lights of the truck. Frank Sinatra's voice was satiny as he sang *Let it Snow! Let it Snow! Let it Snow!*

Jenny sighed, taking in the emotion and sheer romance of the whole day, feeling giddy, hopeful, and so in love. She glanced over at Luke, and he gave her a look filled with love. Jenny wanted to remember this moment for the rest of her life.

CHAPTER 11

THIS FIRST WEEKEND IN DECEMBER, Landis, Mama, Jenny, and Luke had what Landis kept referring to as an *all-hands* meeting in the clearing by the front of the cabins. Jenny snuggled in her puffy coat, grateful for its warmth. At 7:30 in the morning, it was thirty degrees, clear and windy with a light chop on Heron Lake. Mama handed around mugs of steaming coffee. The timer on Jenny's phone binged, and she hurried inside and came back out with paper plates and a basket of fresh-from-the-oven cranberry-orange muffins. Luke tossed the too hot muffin from hand to hand to cool it, and took a large bite. "Good," he mumbled, still chewing, and gave her a thumbs-up.

"Good morning, team. Now we look official," Landis grinned as he handed them each fleecy red ball caps with **Staff, Lakeside Cabins** embroidered on the front in dark green script inside a wreath. Jenny pulled her hat on, liking the feel of it, and looked affectionately at the others who were donning theirs. They all looked bright-eyed and eager to help. Landis smiled at her and gave a little salute. "I'm ceding the floor to our team leader, Jenny."

Jenny pulled a folded up note from her pocket and scanned it. "Let's just review the schedule one more time. This will be our official holiday routine. So our guests today will leave by 11:00. We can't afford to have any late check outs, so we'll need to be nice but firm. Luke, if you and Landis could handle the checking out and the checking in, I'd be grateful. My guess is that the new guests will roll in early because they're excited about Christmas and about being here."

"We've got it." Landis gave a confident smile. The head greeter, affable host, and unofficial mayor of the Lakeside Resort looked like he was in his element.

"Once they're out of the cabins, Mama and I are going to strip dirty beds and clean those cabins like a whirlwind," she said.

"We'll be speedy as jack rabbits," Claire said, a determined glint in her eye.

Jenny went on. "Our new guests checking in will have a chance to relax this afternoon and tonight. Tomorrow night, we'll host the children's choir from St. Elizabeth's. Lily's encouraged the folks coming from the community to carpool, but we'll still need to manage the parking."

Luke held up a hand. "Landis and I have got that covered."

"Great." Jenny paused, a little worried. "Including our guests, we could easily have seventy-five or a hundred people here for the concert, so we need to make sure everybody's comfortable, help out the folks with mobility issues, and keep an eagle eye out for kids who might get too close to the water's edge. This weekend will be a good dry run for the next three." Jenny tucked the note back in her pocket and had an afterthought. "Oh, and let's try to throw Lily and Tom together every opportunity we have."

Luke just shook his head at her, but he was fighting a smile.

"Let each other know if you need anything. I'm so grateful for your help and support." Feeling a wave of love, Jenny gathered in Mama, Landis, and Luke for a group hug.

The men from the party supply outfit arrived promptly at 8:00. Luke reminded them that they had guests staying in the cabins, so they worked quietly and efficiently to erect an elegant- looking large white tent in the clearing. With many large, half-oval walls that were clear, guests could stay warm and still enjoy views of the lake. "The tents are durable, waterproof, and windproof. Gusts from the lake shouldn't give you any trouble," the friendly man in the Kent's Tents jacket told them.

The Kent's Tents men worked on setting up heaters.

When they'd finished connecting lines, Luke and Jenny stepped in the tent to feel how warm it was. It was toasty and comfortable, ideal for tomorrow's performance. The head man patted a heater and gave them a savvy look. "It has 46,000 BTUs and tip-over protection. Fine heaters," he assured them. After he showed them how to adjust the thermostat so they wouldn't overheat the guests or run out of propane, Jenny signed the paperwork, and the men trundled off in their box truck.

Back outside, the cold morning air was bracing. An osprey flew gracefully overhead. Jenny looked around, proud of how appealing and festive the cabins and property looked. "Let's admire our work." Linking her arm in Luke's, the two strolled along the new winding walkway.

"The wreaths look good." Luke tilted his head toward the cabins.

On each of the arched cabin doors hung the fresh balsam wreaths that Mama had made. Simply adorned with pine cones and a red velvet bow, they were rustic and understated, just right for the cabins. "They turned out well," Jenny said. "You men did a good job on the lights, too."

Luke and Landis had strung tiny white lights along the railings of each cabin porch. They sparkled in the morning light, and Jenny loved how they looked. She'd keep them lit day and night, she decided.

A bluebird swooped by them and perched on the branch of a nearby cypress tree. Tilting his head, he seemed to be looking right at them with his intelligent eyes. Bluebirds were her connection to Jax. "Hey, there, Daddy," Jenny called softly to the little bird, feeling a swell of affection for him. "Hope you're doing good. We're swell here, thanks to you. Love this place. Love you."

Luke just smiled, understanding. The two held hands as they walked on.

The choir from St. Elizabeth's was a big hit. Ending the concert was a skinny young boy with an astonishing voice singing *The Little Drummer Boy*. When the last note faded, there was a moment of silence, and then the audience burst into wild applause.

On Saturday, December 14th, Santa was driving down from the North Pole to stop by the Lakeside Resort and visit good girls and boys. Jenny was frazzled. There were so many things that needed to be done. Based on Lily's input, a crowd of parents and kids from the community were ecstatic about coming to see Santa, and they'd be arriving in just over two hours. All Jenny's helpers seemed to either be milling around or heading off in the wrong direction.

Slowly, things began to come together. Because last weekend's guests had been so complimentary about everything, the choir, the decorations, and the air of congenial festivity, Jenny was not worrying quite as hard about this weekend being a success.

Landis and Ashe were painting directional arrow

signs that read, THIS WAY TO SANTA. Though the red and white paint was faded on the little Shasta and wouldn't be painted until Luke got to it in the spring, he and Landis had scrubbed it and strung it with so many red and green lights that it looked sparkly and inviting. Charlotte had added more bling to her thrift store Santa chair, including a gilt frame and white faux fur throws. The velvet chair looked more like a regal throne now, and with white painted plywood temporarily on the floor and the stains and holes in the walls hidden by swaths of white shimmery fabric, the small camper looked enchanting. Children would adore it, and the pictures parents could take would be extra special.

Hugh and Viv, returning guests from Southern Pines, were in the holiday spirit and on board to help. Tall, beefy Hugh was preparing for his upcoming role by walking off a ways and practicing his *Ho, ho, ho's*. Wearing a plush-looking Santa suit that included a stuffed prosthetic belly, his cottony white fluffy beard and brows were realistic, and his genial air made him a perfect Santa. Burbling with enthusiasm, his wife Viv put the final touches on Santa's workshop. In her red velvet dress with the sweetheart neckline, white velvet boots that looked like go-go boots, and a big white Dolly Parton-inspired wig, Viv was a very credible if not slightly sexy-looking Mrs. Claus. Jenny put an arm around her. "Mrs. Claus, you look authentic and a tad foxy."

Viv pretended to fluff her large white wig and laughed

heartily. "I hadn't tried for that look, but at age sixty something, I'll take that compliment in a heartbeat."

Mama was in the Dogwood, borrowing Jenny's color printer for song sheets they'd use at the carol singalong next weekend. Only choosing songs the choirs and choral group were not singing, Mama was copying the music in an extra-large font and adding holly borders.

Jenny was putting final touches on small gift bags they'd prepared for Santa to give the children when she heard a car horn tooting. The faded green sedan with a blinking Santa, sleigh, and reindeer atop it pulled in, Ashe at the wheel.

Looking sun-kissed and exhilarated, the happy couple stepped out waving, their faces radiating happiness. Jenny hurried over to greet them and gave them each fervent hugs. "Welcome home, married people. We missed y'all but knew you were having a grand time."

"We were. We did..." Ashe trailed off, looking as scarlet-faced and shy as if Jenny was asking about their love life.

"How was the over-the-water bungalow?' Jenny asked brightly, throwing Ashe a conversational lifeline since he seemed to need it.

"Cool. Very cool," Ashe said, looking relieved.

"Oh, stellar, glorious, amazeballs," Charlotte said effusively. "The hut had a glass bottom so we could watch the tropical fish swimming under us. We snorkeled and hiked and ate a lot of fresh seafood. It was a splendid honeymoon. I just wanted to live in St. Lucia forever." Charlotte looked rapt at the memory.

"It's always good to get away and even better to get back home," Ashe said, ever the pragmatist.

"So true," Jenny murmured.

Shifting gears, Charlotte rubbed her hands together, her eyes alight. "Let's assign Lily and Tom to direct all the visitors to Santa's little Shasta."

"Good plan." Time to get that romance started. Jenny had texted Charlotte about her matchmaking idea, and her friend was all for it

"I've got an important task for today," Ashe announced, opening the trunk of the car and pulling out an open shotgun. "I'm your man for harvesting mistletoe."

"Good thinking. You need to get the shooting done between these guests checking out and new ones checking in and well before any families arrive," Jenny pointed him in the right direction. "Luke and I scoped out three big balls of mistletoe in the hardwoods on the west side of the cabins. Luke and Landis are going to want to tag along because shooting is involved, and they might need a little help from you now."

"Good. I'll go find those boys." Slipping the shotgun back in the trunk, Ashe strode off.

Charlotte watched him as he walked away and gave a little swoony sigh. "Isn't he just *dashing*? So manly and strong, just like Rhett Butler."

"He is," Jenny agreed, hiding her smile. Always a

gentleman, Ashe reminded her more of an academic or an absentminded professor than a dashing Rhett, but if that's how Charlotte saw him, that worked fine all round.

Taking her friend's hand, Jenny led her toward the Shasta. "Come on, Scarlett. I can't wait to show you our new diamond-in-the-rough vintage camper. You *will* fall in love."

By December 21st, volunteers Lily, Tom, Charlotte, and Ashe wore their own fleecy red *Staff, Lakeside Cabins* ball caps and worked seamlessly with the others. Crack shot Ashe had provided them with a large bucket of fresh mistletoe. Tying sprigs together with white velvet ribbon, Jenny passed sprigs out to delighted guests. Charlotte had cornered Lily and Tom, and safety-pinned large clumps to the brims of their ball caps, telling them gruffly, "It's required."

Pink-cheeked Tom looked bemused as he slipped back on his hat, and Lily looked shyly at him from under her hat brim as the two of them headed off, walking closely together. Jenny hid a grin and shot Charlotte a look. Her friend was silently mouthing *Yay* and holding up two fists in a silent cheer.

For Jenny, the one mystery of the last weekend of the whole Christmas extravaganza was the horse-drawn wagon that was scheduled for that very afternoon. Luke claimed he had it covered, but when she'd pressed him for details, he put a finger to the side of his nose and nodded just like Santa did before he rose up the chimney. "All will be revealed," he said cryptically.

Jenny knew she could be a perfectionist and a bit of a controller, so she tried to let it go, but she worried about it. If Luke couldn't pull off the horse-drawn wagon slash sleigh ride, guests would be crushed and start writing those awful reviews online and... Catching herself catastrophizing, Jenny made herself take the dogs and Levi for a long, brisk walk.

In his brand new Santa suit, Garland the goose was a popular draw for all the guests. Kids would lie right down on the ground to get close to Garland and beg their parents to take a picture.

Midday, in the lull between the time that the last guests had reluctantly checked out and the new guests checked in, Jenny and Luke were in the driveway shoveling gravel into a pothole that seemed to have sprung up overnight. Hearing a sound she couldn't identify, Jenny stopped shoveling, putting a hand up to shield her eyes from the sun as she peered down the road.

A long red wagon drawn by two magnificent gray dappled horses creaked and jingled as it drew into view. Jenny drew in a breath sharply. The handsome horses were tall, muscular, and proud looking. Sleigh bells were draped across their withers, and the horses' manes were threaded with red ribbons. The wide-planked wooden wagon they were pulling looked vintage, and it was decorated with two large wreaths and red bows. The whole scene was straight out of Currier and Ives. Jenny put her hands on her cheeks, delighted.

But the biggest surprise was the driver. Holding the reins lightly was a man in a top hat, a black overcoat, and a red scarf tied jauntily around his neck. When he drew nearer, he raised a hand and gave a jubilant but crooked smile. Jenny smiled back, close to tears. "Your Daddy," she said wonderingly and looked at Luke.

"Yup," Luke said proudly, as his father brought the horses to a stop and tipped his hat at them.

"You all are so good-looking. How did you find us such a handsome rig, Frank?" Jenny called as Luke took the horses' harnesses and Frank stepped down.

"It's a t-t-tobacco wagon just like the ones my daddy used to use t-t-to haul bales to auction. One of my buddies fixed it up and l-l-lent us these beauties," Frank said proudly, gently laying his hand on the side of one the horses.

"Those two horses are spectacular," Jenny breathed, taking in their powerful-looking muscles and the sheer mass of them.

"They're Percherons, draft horses known for being smart and hard workers. They're called the gentle giants," Luke said.

"May I bring Levi over to meet them?" Jenny asked, guessing that her mini would come up to these big guys' knees but be ecstatic to meet equine friends.

"Of c-c-course," Frank said with a magnanimous wave.

Each musical performance was well-received. Although Jenny had written checks to the churches and groups who were performing, Mama had stood up after each performance, sweetly asked for a small donation for the churches and organizations performing, and passed around a red basket. Jenny would never forget the looks of gratitude on the choir directors' faces when Mama handed them the large stack of bills.

On Christmas Eve, Jenny and Luke headed over to the clearing where the caroling would take place. Landis had stoked up a roaring bonfire, and Mama was wearing a coat and a red Santa's cap. Tom and Lily were cuing up Landis's iPod and speakers. Bundled up warmly, guests' breath froze and their faces glowed as they gathered around the fire and looked over the sheet music Mama had handed out.

Remembering that she'd left defrosting steaks on the counter, Jenny hurried back to the Dogwood to check on them. Buddy and Bear would relish that snack, but inside all was quiet and the steaks were untouched. The dogs were napping by the woodstove, and Levi was snuggled in his cedar bed, his eyes at half-mast. To be on the safe side, Jenny slipped the plate of sirloins into the micro-wave oven.

The blue of the laptop screen caught Jenny's eye, though. Before closing it down, Jenny saw the order that

Luke had accidentally left up and broke into a slow smile. Her fiancé was getting her a bat box for Christmas. Jenny read the gift card he'd written to enclose.

Jen, The mosquitoes were fierce this summer. Here's a nontoxic way to keep them away. One bat can eat up to a thousand mosquitoes per hour. All my love forever, Luke

Jenny was impressed with the thousand bugs per hour fact, but she read the *All my love forever* three times and found she was blinking back tears. The man would never be a smooth-talking Romeo, but what girl wanted that? Luke was a grounded, steady guy who adored her. Though he didn't wear his feelings on his sleeve, Luke felt things deeply. He cherished her, and he was everything she'd ever wanted.

Jenny closed out the screen and headed outside. It was no secret that his other gift to her was a camper-sized version of a luxury comfort bed, a big help for her tricky back—and other things—when they set off on their honeymoon camping adventure this June. Romantic as all get out when she thought about it.

Jenny had to laugh. She was getting as practical and possibly nerdy as Luke was. Her Christmas gifts to him were new tires for the Shasta and a high-tech weather station that could be mounted on a pole to thoroughly, almost professionally, track the weather. With hygrometers, solar panels, lightning detectors, and a humidity gauge, it was a solid gift for an outdoors guy who liked techie stuff.

Jenny joined the others. Slipping in front of Luke, she leaned back into him, and he reached around her shoulders and gave her a hug.

When Tom hit the play button, the powerful iPod speakers emanated the clear opening chords to *Oh, Come All Ye Faithful*. Guests adjusted reading glasses, held their song sheets in gloved hands, and began to sing along.

Those who were self-conscious about their voices sang softly or mouthed the words at first, but as the song went on, guests' voices swelled and even the bashful joined in with feeling. By the time they launched into *It Came upon a Midnight Clear*, the carolers' voices were even stronger. *Silent Night, Holy Night* was sung with pure reverence as guests standing in a clear and cold night lit with stars imagined another starlit night in Bethlehem.

As the last note faded, Jenny leaned back into Luke's solid bulk and closed her eyes for a moment, sending up a prayer of thanks for the love she had in her life and for the many miracles of Christmas. Opening her eyes, Jenny turned and leveled a gaze at Luke. "Love you more than you know," she murmured.

Luke gave her a slow, sweet smile and pulled her close. "Merry Christmas, darlin' girl."

A Special Invitation

Dear Reader,

Thank you so much for reading *Mistletoe at the Lakeside Resort* and spending time with me at Heron Lake. Hope you loved this book.

I need your help!

Reader reviews are the most powerful tool for making my book successful. While the story is fresh on your mind, would you please go to Amazon and write a review?

As always, I'm grateful for your support.
Susan Schild

ABOUT THE AUTHOR

USA Today Bestselling author Susan Schild writes heartwarming novels about heroines over age forty having adventures, falling in love and finding their happily ever afters.

A wife and stepmother, Susan enjoys reading and taking walks with her Labrador retriever mixes, Tucker and Gracie. She and her family live in North Carolina.

Susan has used her professional background as a psychotherapist and management consultant to add authenticity to her characters.

For early word about new releases, follow Susan on BookBub: https://bit.ly/2tHuDzu

You can also learn more about Susan's other books by following her on her Amazon Author Page: https://amzn.to/2T5CS7F

LOOK FOR MY NEXT BOOK

Reader friends, mark your calendars! *A Wedding at the Lakeside Resort*, Book 4 in The Lakeside Resort Series will be released in June of 2020. Look for more friendship, fun, inn-keeping mishaps, romantic road trips in the Airstream, and a dreamy wedding!

For alerts about new releases, follow Susan
on BookBub: https://bit.ly/2tHuDzu

OTHER BOOKS BY AUTHOR SUSAN SCHILD

If you enjoyed this book, you'll be sure to enjoy the other books in *The Lakeside Resort* Series!

Christmas at the Lakeside Resort
(The Lakeside Resort Series Book 1)

Love and Adventures after 40

Forty-two year old Jenny Beckett is dreading the holidays. Her fiancé has just called off their Christmas wedding, and she's been evicted from her darling chicken coop cottage. When her estranged father dies and leaves her eight rustic guest cabins on Heron Lake, Jenny seizes the chance to make a new life. She packs up her dogs, her miniature horse and her beat up Airstream trailer and moves to the lake.

Short on time and money, Jenny and her contractor, widower Luke, work feverishly to renovate the cabins in time for the festive holiday event she's promised her very first guests. When an unexpected blizzard snows them in and jeopardizes the resort's opening, Jenny and Luke work to save the event and, along the way, find true love… and the magic of Christmas.

Summer at the Lakeside Resort
(The Lakeside Resort Series Book 2)

Ready for more love and adventure after 40?

Forty-three year old Jenny Beckett has just renovated eight rustic guest cabins on beautiful Heron Lake, North Carolina. Brand new to the inn keeping business, she is struggling to make The Lakeside Resort profitable. Wrangling guests like The Fighting Couple, persnickety attorneys, and the curvy gals from the Fabulous You Fitness Week keep her on her toes.

Jenny's business isn't her only problem. Her mother and stepfather have just moved in for an extended stay. Startling developments with her possible fiancé, Luke, make Jenny question his commitment to her. An all-gal camping trip in her old Airstream lifts her spirits, but Jenny still has doubts about whether she and Luke can make their love work. After all the heartache she's had, can Jenny learn to trust love again and finally find her happily ever after?

And check out my Willow Hill series as well!

Linny's Sweet Dream List
(A Willow Hill Novel Book 1)

Set in the off-beat Southern town of Willow Hill, North Carolina, Susan Schild's moving and witty novel tells of one woman who loses everything — and finds more than she ever expected.

At thirty-eight, Linny Taylor is suddenly living a life she thought only happened to other, more careless people. Widowed for the second time, and broke, thanks to her cheating late husband, Linny has no house, no job, and no options except to go back home. There, in a trailer as run down as her self-esteem, Linny makes a list of things that might bring happiness. A porch swing. A job that nourishes her heart as well as her bank balance. Maybe even a date or two.

At first, every goal seems beyond reach. But it's hard for Linny to stay in the doldrums when a stray puppy is coercing her out of her shell—right into the path of the town's kind, compassionate vet. The quirky town is filled with friends and family, including Linny's mother, Dottie, who knows more about heartache than her daughters ever guessed. And as Linny contemplates each item on her list, she begins to realize that the dreams most worth holding on to can only be measured in the sweetness of a life lived to the fullest...

Sweet Carolina Morning
(A Willow Hill Novel Book 2)

Life down South just got a whole lot sweeter in Susan Schild's new novel about a woman whose happily-ever-after is about to begin...whether she's ready for it or not.

Finally, just shy of forty years old, Linny Taylor is living the life of her dreams in her charming hometown of Willow Hill, North Carolina. The past few years have been anything but a fairy tale: Left broke by her con man late-husband, Linny has struggled to rebuild her life from scratch. Then she met Jack Avery, the town's much-adored veterinarian. *And she's marrying him.*

Everything should be coming up roses for Linny. So why does she have such a serious case of pre-wedding jitters? It could be because Jack's prosperous family doesn't approve of her rough-and-tumble background. Or that his ex-wife is suddenly back on the scene. Or that Linny has yet to win over his son's heart. All these obstacles — not to mention what she should *wear* when she walks down the aisle — are taking the joy out of planning her wedding. Linny better find a way to trust love again, or she might risk losing the one man she wants to be with — forever…

Sweet Southern Hearts
(A Willow Hill Novel Book 3)

Welcomes you back to the offbeat Southern town of Willow Hill, North Carolina, for a humorous, heartwarming story of new beginnings, do-overs, and self-discovery…

When it comes to marriage, third time's the charm for Linny Taylor. She's thrilled to be on her honeymoon with Jack Avery, Willow Hill's handsome veterinarian. But just like the hair-raising white water rafting trip Jack persuades her to take, newlywed life has plenty of dips and bumps.

Jack's twelve-year-old son is resisting all Linny's efforts

to be the perfect stepmother, while her own mother, Dottie, begs her to tag along on the first week of a free-wheeling RV adventure. Who knew women "of a certain age" could drum up so much trouble? No sooner is Linny sighing with relief at being back home than she's helping her frazzled sister with a new baby...and dealing with an unexpected legacy from her late ex. Life is fuller—and richer—than she ever imagined, but if there's one thing Linny's learned by now, it's that there's always room for another sweet surprise...